"YOU O[...]"

The students[...] [...]si-
tive to the nuances of professorial mood
changes, shifted in their seats and waited
for me to speak.

"No, I am not okay." I inhaled and continued, "I have just learned that, according
to an autopsy ordered by the family, Dr.
Garcia was poisoned." I pointed to the article in the paper I clutched in my hand.
"And," I plunged on in spite of a few
gasps, "the police are holding a student for
questioning."

I sat down and took a long gulp from my
water bottle and then, in the stunned silence that greeted my words, I began slowly
fanning my face with the folded newspaper.
It was time to regroup. I heard myself say,
"Let's come together in a circle now. What
do you make of this dreadful news?"

THE "M" WORD

A Bel Barrett Mystery

JANE ISENBERG

AVON

TWILIGHT

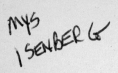

MYS
ISENBERG

This is a work of fiction. Names, characters, places, and incidents either
are the product of the author's imagination or are used fictitiously. Any
resemblance to actual events, locales, organizations, or persons, living or
dead, is entirely coincidental and beyond the intent of either the author or
the publisher.

AVON BOOKS, INC.
1350 Avenue of the Americas
New York, New York 10019

Copyright © 1999 by Jane Isenberg
Inside cover author photo by Susan Tompkins
Published by arrangement with the author
Library of Congress Catalog Card Number: 98-93548
ISBN: 0-380-80280-5
www.avonbooks.com/twilight

First Avon Twilight Printing: March 1999

AVON TWILIGHT TRADEMARK REG. U.S. PAT. OFF. AND IN OTHER COUN-
TRIES, MARCA REGISTRADA, HECHO EN U.S.A.

Printed in the U.S.A.

WCD   10   9   8   7   6   5   4   3   2   1

In memory of
Corinne G. Levin
Inspiring educator, loving friend

Acknowledgments

Hillary's right. It takes a whole village to nurture a baby, and this book is, in many ways, my baby. Some whose wisdom and insight have been helpful are Hubert Babinski, Elaine Foster, Roberto Gutierrez, Dr. Annette Hollander, Dr. Shelly Kolton, Juan Marte, Jan Marks, John Mayher, Luis Medina, Paco Padim, Susan Price, Joan Rafter, Susan Ruskin, Denise Stybr, Paul Tompkins, and Ruth and David Tait. I'm indebted to Barbara Jaye Wilson, Pat Carlson, and Barbara Paul and my other Sisters-in-Crime for both inspiration and example. And I'm grateful to Rachel Isenberg for her witty suggestions, to Brian Stoner for creative problem solving, to Daniel Isenberg for sensitive feedback, and, of course, to my husband, Phil Tompkins, for computer help, "site inspections," and good-humored support.

Another "M" word is *midwives*, and it took several of these to enable me to give birth to this book. So a big, loud postpartum thanks to Laura Blake Peterson, my agent, and to Jennifer Sawyer Fisher, my editor. And finally, thanks to my wise, caring, and patient writing group, Susan Babinski, Pat Juell, and Rebecca Mlynarczyk, as well as to my savvy and tactful friend, Dinah Stevenson.

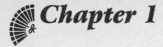

Chapter 1

To: Bbarrett@circle.com
Subject: Red Hot Mama
Date: Fri, 14 Oct 1994 06:39:59
From: Rbarrett@UWash.edu

Mom,

What do you mean you're on-line with a "menopause support group"? How'd you find it? What did you do, just surf the Net until you hit a chat room where everybody was sweating? Or don't you remember? Is it like an on-line twelve-step program? Do you have to use your real name? If you want to know how I felt when you e-mailed me about this, remember how you lost it when Mark got his tongue stud?

Good news! I finally got my hours at the restaurant changed, so I just work nights, and since all my classes are during the day, now I've got a really sweet schedule.

Gotta hit the books. Hope all your students are brilliant this semester. That Fall Festival doesn't sound so bad. You should go. Remember, all work and no play, etc. Keith says hi. Call me soon. I miss you.

Love,
Rebecca

P.S. Oh yeah, I used your credit card Tuesday to bail my car out after it got towed, but don't worry, I'll pay you back.

The goddamn Fall Festival turned out to be what my son Mark would call "kick-ass," so I was glad I'd let Rebecca nudge me into going. For starters, I ran into Sarah Wolf, an old friend who covers the education beat for the *Jersey City Herald*. We met years ago in an aerobics class at the Y. Since we were grayer and rounder than our classmates, we bonded quickly. And our friendship evolved into one long conversation, which we pick up whenever we meet. I am so fond of Sarah that I have almost forgiven her for becoming a grandmother before me.

That night Sarah was half hidden behind a paper plate piled with flan, sweet potato pie, and chocolate truffles. And behind the plate I could see the unmistakable bulge of a Snugli and the dimpled cheek of Sarah's first grandchild, Hannah. My inner grandmother was green with envy. Struggling to repress this unworthy response, I grinned and said, "Hi Sarah. You look like a walking mirage." We hugged carefully, reaching over and around both her stash of goodies and the sleeping infant.

"Here, help save me from myself," Sarah offered, pushing the plate in my direction. "The pounds don't drop so easily anymore. So what do you think? Isn't she precious?"

"An absolute love lump," I answered, trying not to drool on Hannah as I bent over the Snugli for a closer ogle. "She's so succulent. Who does she look like?" I asked, popping a truffle into my mouth.

"Like her grandma of course," Sarah replied with a decidedly complacent chuckle. "Seriously, Bel, you're going to love being a grandmother."

Like I need convincing, I thought, trying to persuade my inner grandmother that kidnapping Hannah was not an option.

Sarah was saying, "And speaking of the people who are going to make this transformation possible, the people who hold the keys to your immortality, what do you hear from Rebecca? And how's Mark?" Sarah was adjusting the baby's position with her free hand while she talked, and Hannah, still sound asleep, snorted a soft baby snort.

"Rebecca's fine, but making me a grandmother is a very low-level priority for her now. She lives and breathes to get into physical therapy school. And her boyfriend is no way ready."

Sarah laughed again and said, "Well, Jan and Peter weren't ready either, and just look what we have here." With that, Sarah buried her nose in Hannah's neck and made cooing and gurgling noises.

"So what about Mark? What's up with him?" Sarah shifted the Snugli again.

"Same old same old," I replied, gently patting the Snugli. "Nannying, evening classes. He sees a lot of Sienna still, but he insists they're just friends, whatever that means."

"Well, before too long, you'll have one of these, I promise," said Sarah, stroking Hannah's cheek with two fingers.

I didn't want to argue with Sarah. Instead I said, "She sure is a sound sleeper. Look at her. She's totally oblivious to the music and the mobs of people here."

"She sure is," Sarah murmured, staring besottedly at the baby. Then in her regular voice she added, "This really is quite a do."

"I know. Can you believe it? It's River Edge Community College's first ever major fund-raiser. I never imagined a turnout like this," I added, relieving Sarah of yet another truffle. "I almost didn't come."

"You're kidding?" replied Sarah. "Why not? RECC's resident workaholic have too many term papers to read?"

"Well, now that you mention it, Grandma, yes. But also I just wasn't up for it. I mean, really, Sarah. Just what I didn't want to do on a Friday night was drag myself out to make nice to every political hack between Guttenberg and Bayonne who's looking for a free meal."

"Oh Bel. You're just bitter because all the best-looking ones are in jail now," Sarah quipped. I was relieved that grandmotherhood had not damaged Sarah's sense of humor. "Actually, I didn't want to come either because I'd promised the kids I'd baby-sit so they could have a night out. Then I remembered this assignment, so here we both are. It's been a while since I chased down a story with a kid in tow."

I couldn't help smiling. "I see you've made the transition from backpack to Snugli. Very nineties, Sarah." I could feel my smile disappear as I continued, "I really don't know what the hell I'm doing here. This is the year I was going to pull back from a lot of RECC activities."

"Oh Bel. Give me a break. You've said that every year since I've known you. Tell me"—Sarah looked serious in spite of a mouthful of flan—"who dreamed up this festival anyway?" She held up her fork as I was about to answer. "No. Silly me. This whole thing has to have been the brainchild of Salvadoran super-woman and RECC's president, Dr. Altagracia Garcia, right?"

I nodded, and before I could elaborate, Sarah went on, now rocking from side to side, cradling the Snugli with one arm as she swayed. "I figured as much, even though somebody tried to tell me the RECC Development Committee planned it." Now she was struggling to impale a particularly gooey morsel of sweet potato pie on her fork as she spoke.

"I don't care what anyone says, the RECC Development Committee had nothing to do with this event. Trust me," I told Sarah, speaking through what I swore to myself would be my last mouthful of truffle. "All the credit for this festival's success goes to Dr. G. She was the one who invited local officials . . ." I had to stop talking to scrape up a tiny glop of flan with Sarah's fork.

"The woman is amazing. I see that she even got a few folks from the governor's office to show up." Sarah took advantage of my feeding frenzy to add her own observation on the scene. "Who got so many area eateries involved?" she asked, pointing to the rapidly diminishing pile of goodies on her plate.

"Dr. G did that too," I answered. "Politicos and restaurateurs actually agreed to provide samples of favorite recipes or free meals that she's going to auction off."

"Wow." I could tell Sarah was impressed because she had stopped eating and rocking and was gazing at the crowd. Little Hannah stirred in her cocoon, and her translucent eyelids fluttered.

Resisting the urge to brush butterfly kisses onto Hannah's tiny cheek, I added, "Yes. Persuading them to buy into this affair was impressive, but her best move was having the festival here in Liberty State Park. Don't you think so, Hannah?" I was leaning over the Snugli again, savoring the scent of talcum and baby's breath.

"Yes. They did a fabulous job renovating this train

station, and, of course, you can't beat the view of the Manhattan skyline from here." Sarah resumed rocking, so I straightened up.

"Absolutely. Against the backdrop of the Big Apple and Ms. Liberty, even a dog fight would take on a special glow." I paused and then added, "Dr. G is amazing. You know, Sarah, she's actually convinced me that someday RECC will move out of our decrepit rented facilities in downtown Jersey City to a state-of-the-art waterfront site. Then she says we'll be a kind of Harvard-on-the-Hudson."

"Let's face it, Bel. She sold you a bill of goods you wanted to buy, right? You still haven't given up on having a river view from your office, have you?" Sarah's tone was light, but I could tell from the pitying look in her eye that she thought I was a hopeless dreamer. She was pretty cynical for a grandmother.

"No, I guess I haven't." I was not going to apologize for wishing. "Check her out."

We stood there together watching Dr. G make her way through the crowd. "Who's that woman trailing Dr. Garcia?" asked Sarah.

"That's Betty Ramsey, her executive assistant. I'm surprised you haven't run into her. Betty monitors Dr. G's every move. God, Sarah! Would you look at that parade of men following them? The RECC trustees, a couple of deans, a couple of commissioners!"

"Hey, I can't blame them. Dr. Garcia's really in fine form tonight," were Sarah's next words as the object of our attention moved gracefully down the aisles of food-covered tables. A stunning raven-haired woman of thirty-something wearing a lime green suit and matching stiletto heels, RECC's president was smiling, shaking hands, tasting, and chatting, first in English, then in Spanish. Sarah was right. Dr. G was in fine form. She looked great.

"Look at Betty. We're eating bonbons and she's running her middle-aged tail off trying to micromanage Dr. G." Laughing, I pointed my chocolatey index finger in the direction of the stocky, dark-skinned figure following my glamorous boss.

"Well, Virginia, you may be right about Santa after all," Sarah said with a grin. "If she can pull off a major event like this, Altagracia Garcia is going to make a big difference at RECC. Who knows? Maybe she'll even get you your waterfront campus. Anyway, it's about time RECC had a woman president to whip the place into shape, right, sweetie?" Sarah had addressed part of this question to Hannah, who answered with another faint snort. I was disappointed when, abruptly handing me the now nearly empty paper plate, Sarah said, "Here, finish these. I've gotta go do my Brenda Starr bit now. 'Cause when this little girl wakes up, we want to be home, don't we, Hannah? I'll call you, Bel." And blowing me an air kiss, Sarah disappeared into the throng.

After Sarah and Hannah abandoned me, I continued enjoying the scene in spite of the fact that I was having a hot flash just about every ten minutes. One was particularly uncomfortable. While the preauction tasting was still in full swing, I started to sweat. I tried to look casual as I pushed through the crowd to the door. It's not easy to look casual with your blouse stuck to your skin and your whole head dripping wet.

When I finally escaped, I practically ran to the railing overlooking the river. I couldn't find my fan, so I fished a Kleenex out of my purse and mopped my face and neck. Thanks to the breeze coming off the

Hudson, I began to feel a little cooler. And there was that Manhattan skyline just a river's width away. In case you haven't guessed, I'm a sucker for that string of skyscrapers.

Standing there gazing at the lights, I automatically started doing my kegels. My friend Wendy swore to me on her dog-eared copy of *Ourselves Growing Older* that repeatedly contracting the unpronounceable muscle that stops voluntary urination would give me more bladder control, so I wouldn't pee every time I sneeze or laugh. At first I was, to say the least, skeptical. But I'll do anything to keep out of diapers for another decade or two, so I've been trying to integrate kegels into my lifestyle. How the hell I'm supposed to do fifty or more a day and earn a living is still a mystery to me. Anyway, I was only up to about fourteen for the whole day, so I just stood there, contracting and enjoying the crisp air and the view.

There were a few other people standing at intervals along the fence staring across the river. Without my glasses, I didn't recognize any of them, even the man closest to me. Apparently he had just taken off his own glasses because he wiped them and stashed them in his jacket pocket. Then, glancing my way, he recognized me. Walking toward me he stopped a few feet away. Only then could I make out the chiseled features of Commissioner Thomas Koladnar. He snapped to attention in an exaggerated double take, gave me a mock salute, and said, "My favorite River Edge Community College faculty member, Professor Sibyl Barrett, how are you? Still charming people into your classroom and working your wiles on them?"

I hoped he couldn't see my cheeks flush. He looks just like a young Paul Newman. Really, he's got the same sturdy build and low-key dimples. Suddenly I was aware that I probably looked like a human sponge. So forgetting the kegels, I sucked in my gut and smoothed back my hair. I was flattered by his enthusiastic greeting, but just for a moment. Before I got too carried away, I reminded myself that Koladnar is, after all, a politician, and from Hudson County to boot.

As a native of New Jersey, I've always known that Hudson County politicians are a special breed. They believe in family values. When we moved to Hoboken, the superintendent of schools had five relatives employed by the Board of Education. They value friendship. Jersey City officials rewarded loyal, if untalented, friends with jobs in local schools until the state took over the school system. They really believe in our right to vote. In fact, it's a standing joke here that to vote only once in a single election is evidence of poor citizenship. Finally, they uphold tradition. The machine politics fighting to survive here in the nineties date back to the notorious Frank "I Am the Law" Hague, mayor of Jersey City, whose reign lasted from 1917 to 1947.

To be fair, though, Tom Koladnar is a member of a new generation of Jersey City pols. He's young, educated, and aware of how the latest wave of immigrants, gentrification, and development are transforming his turf. And he's sharp. How I envy his politician's memory for names and faces! Of course, until his allusion to his visit last year to my Cultures and Values class, I'd forgotten all about it. But I'd persuaded him to come, and he'd given a talk, something about immigrants and American culture. Since many of my students are recent immigrants, they were mesmerized.

"Chilly? Want my jacket?"

Just as he said that, of course, I felt another surge of heat burn my cheeks. Let's face it, I haven't been "chilly" in ages. My response poured out in a rush as if I were a schoolgirl. "No thanks. I came out to get some air. Isn't this a splendid spot? I'd sure hate to see it turned into a golf course. I fantasize about having my daughter's wedding here."

I mean, why the hell was I telling him about my fantasies? Koladnar ignored my dig about his proposal to develop the riverbank haven into a golf course. In case you haven't guessed, I love Liberty State Park just as it is, a refuge for migrating birds and small wildlife as well as for joggers, cyclists, picnickers, and walkers like me and my friend Wendy. Koladnar turned away from the view and smiled at me. He looked into my eyes, saying, "Your daughter's getting married? Congratulations!"

"Oh no." By this time I was stammering. "I mean, Rebecca's living with her boyfriend in Seattle, but they don't have any definite plans." I heard myself babbling, "It's just that it's so beautiful here. I can picture them waltzing . . . But that's only Jewish mother talk."

"Give them time. You'll be dancing at their wedding soon enough. Want to join me?" He offered me his arm. "I'm going back to peddle my pirogi at the food auction. What we elected officials have to do these days to stay in office." He flashed me a grin that shifted all those dimples around and back, and I caught a glimpse of the gleam in his blue eyes. Politician or not, he is disarming. "But selling those suckers is going to be easy. Have you tried them?"

"Yes and they're delicious. As good as Tania's." This was high praise since pirogis from Tania's, a fixture in downtown Jersey City, are to die for.

"That's because they're from Tania's, but don't tell." He winked again, this time as if we were both in on the scam, and squeezed my arm in farewell. Then he turned and walked back toward the crowd in the nearby building, leaving me shaking my head. Wouldn't you know? The notion of the cagey commissioner passing off his store-bought pirogis as homemade went a long way toward restoring my initial cynicism.

Alone again, I leaned against the fence counting kegels and pondering the evening in progress. The terminal's enormous hall had been totally transformed. Long food-covered tables were decorated with sprays of autumn leaves and polished gourds. Wearing the white toques and black-and-white checked pants of professional chefs, our Culinary Arts students were ladling and slicing for all they were worth. Local bands took turns filling the chamber with salsa, merengues, and blues. Paintings, mostly large abstract splashes of primary colors by area artists, made a vibrant backdrop for the whole scene. It really was quite a party.

Suddenly I trembled. First I sensed and then I actually saw the silhouette of a gray rat moving in the shadows between the fence and the dark water. So very quickly I followed Koladnar back into the railroad station. From the edge of the crowd, I recognized lots of students and some alums.

I was surprised to see Oscar Beckman in full Culinary Arts Institute regalia, serving punch. I had had Oscar in Speech 101 last spring until he was caught cheating on a Restaurant Sanitation II exam in March and suspended by the Discipline Committee for the rest of the semester. He must have sensed my eyes on him because he looked up, and seeing me, he smiled a little uncertainly. I went over to him exclaiming, "Oscar! How good to see you back!" And I really was glad. Oscar's intensity and offbeat humor have always reminded me of my son Mark. It's not just that they have the same tattoos.

"Glad to be back. I think I'll make it this time. I'm gonna have to take Speech again. You teachin' it next semester?" I nodded, and when I told him to come and see me in my office before registration, his wavering smile crystallized into a grin. I recalled again what a hard time I'd had getting too angry with Oscar even when he showed no interest in his classmates' speeches. But, I have to confess, I'm always flattered when a student wants to take a second course with me.

After Oscar filled my paper cup with punch, I contemplated my own attack on the displays of tempting food. Just because I had already sampled dessert and pirogis was no reason I couldn't try some other delicacies. Who would know? After all, Dr. G, who probably weighed in at all of one hundered pounds, was still munching and kibitzing her way among the tables.

Then before my superego could check in with a reminder that I weigh in at considerably more than Dr. G, RECC's president stopped in her tracks. A plate full of food slid from her hand as she clutched her throat. She appeared to be gasping, choking. Betty Ramsey's square frame pulled up short behind her, setting up a domino effect in the retinue. I just gaped, standing there slack-jawed. Dr. Garcia slowly doubled over, her limbs twitching convulsively as she collapsed onto the floor.

I heard Betty's shriek "Help! Hurry! Help!" ring through the terminal, harsh even against the amplified salsa vibrating in the background. Thank God Tom Koladnar got to her side in seconds. Knocking over several trays of food and pushing people back, he and board president Dominic Tarantello and a few others cleared a space around the figure now contorted on the floor.

I just stood there, gripping my paper cup of punch and staring at the spot where Dr. Altagracia Garcia had stood. Then, of course, I began to sweat.

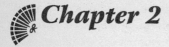 **Chapter 2**

To: Menopausesupportgroup@powersurge.com
Subject: "The ravell'd sleave of care"
Date: Sat, 15 Oct 1994 02:16:19
From: Bbarrett@circle.com

A few hours ago at a fund-raiser the president of the college where I teach collapsed thirty feet away from me. They took her to the hospital in an ambulance. A friend just called to tell me that she's dead. I can't believe it. She was only thirty-six, a talented, hardworking, idealistic woman, the happily married mother of a fourteen-year-old boy. I liked her.

It's 2 a.m. Of course, I can't sleep. If I'm not sweating, I'm picturing her collapsing in convulsions. How will our students feel? They worshipped her. They really counted on her to transform RECC into a place where they could get the education they need to make their futures secure. This will be very hard for them. It's hard for me too. She was a real friend to the faculty, a working intellectual with the starry eyes of a saint. Sure she was a workaholic. In fact, that's probably what killed her. The last time I saw her, I told her to slow down, but at her age, who slows down? RECC is such a stressful place anyway.

Everybody knows stress really exaggerates menopausal symptoms. I've been having heart palpitations for over a year. Believe me, tonight's events haven't helped. My heartbeat is so fast and loud right now just sitting here at the computer. I feel like I'm in an echo chamber with the bass drummer from hell. I wish I could forget the image of this woman collapsing. But I only forget what I want to remember, kind of reverse Freud, you know? Any ideas on how to deal with stress during menopause? I think death is beyond stress. It's traumatic. I've gone from PMS to post-traumatic stress.

"Sorry I'm late. I couldn't leave work till old man Jenkins got in." Frank O'Leary strode past me en route to his preferred seat next to the window in the back of the room. He had been a few minutes late for almost every Intro to Lit class since the semester started because his boss at the pharmacy took extended lunch hours. Frank lowered his rangy six-foot form into the spindly plastic chair. Once settled, he usually looked up at me with a smirky smile as if challenging me to engage his interest. Usually I smiled back, for Frank was a promising student with an analytical bent. But just a few days after Dr. G's death, he was glowering, and I couldn't muster up more than a nod of recognition.

Wordlessly I handed Frank copies of the newspaper articles I had just distributed. They would serve as our text for part of the three-hour class. It seemed appropriate to suspend our consideration of *Macbeth* so students could share their grief and concern.

I knew most of their information would be straight from the rumor mill, so I gave them a few minutes to read Sarah Wolf's straightforward account of how Dr. G had collapsed at the Fall Festival and been pronounced dead on her arrival at the Jersey City Medical Center. I also read aloud and gave out copies of a memo from the Board of Trustees inviting the college community to a memorial service on Friday. Then, struggling to sound matter-of-fact, I said, "Now form your usual discussion groups, please, and let's talk about how President Garcia's death makes us feel and what we remember about her."

As I spoke, they began dragging their seats into clusters of four or five. Rowanda Roberts edged into the room, out of breath, her hunched shoulders and downcast eyes making her look like a walking apology. When she had assumed her place in her group, I gave her the newspaper articles. She smiled a thank-you and murmured, "Sorry I'm late. My baby-sitter, she late."

I moved from group to group, eavesdropping and occasionally facilitating discussion. Rowanda may have been last to arrive, but she was the first to speak in her group. "I only saw her once when I went to graduation last year. I wanted to see what it would be like when time came for my graduation. Anyway, she was nice-lookin'. I liked how she told about her childhood when she first came to this country and worked in the factory and how tough things was. She seem pretty tough too, like when she say she want us all to roll up our sleeves and work hard. She promise to help this college get a campus with a cafeteria and a daycare center. She say she went to school when her son was small so she know how it feel. My son, he don' like to stay with my girlfriend when I come here. He bored at her house. What about her son? Who gonna take care of him now?"

"The boy's father will look after him, I'm sure," I interjected in what I hoped was a reassuring tone. I hoped I was right, too. I'd seen the dashing Javier Garcia only once at Dr. G's first Convocation at RECC.

Rowanda nodded, registering this information, but her brow remained furrowed. I knew she didn't believe me. Her son's father was in jail now, and he hadn't been too attentive before that.

Concepcion Rojas folded and refolded the memo about the memorial service. Acknowledging Rowanda's concern with a glance, she spoke slowly, "It's good they're canceling classes on Friday so we can go to the memorial service for Dr. Garcia. At my job in the rehab center, I work with a lot of pople who lost a loved one. Especially lately with AIDS. I tell them to cry and talk about the person. It's so important to grieve. I try to get them to take it one day at a time. It is good for the whole college to come together as a community and mourn our loss. We'll have to take it one day at a time too."

Concepcion looked straight at Frank, Rowanda, and Loritza Ramirez before going on, and then, taking a deep breath, she continued. "When I was addicted something like this would throw me, but now I can accept it. Death is part of life. The Lord giveth and the Lord taketh away. But why would the Lord take away somebody like Dr. Garcia? She did a lot for this college. She was like me, a Hispanic woman who came to this country for a better life. She was young too, around my age. I'm going to pray for her."

Frank's voice was harsh and strident when he responded to the older woman's solemn words. "Hey, Connie, you better pray for all of us. I can't believe I'm going to have to miss classes again on Friday. I've missed chem lab three times so far this semester. The first two weeks there was still no teacher, and when they finally got a teacher, old man Jenkins said I *had* to work that Friday afternoon. Now the president dies and they're going to cancel classes to have a memorial service?" He brandished the memo in one hand, and then crumpled it in his fist. "Great. I know I sound cold, but I'm trying to transfer to State at the end of this semester. Let's face it, how can I learn that stuff without the class? I wouldn't mind so much if it was a lit class that got canceled. All we do in here is talk about books anyway."

For the first time since I'd learned that Dr. Garcia had died, my lips twitched in what would surely have become a smile if the door hadn't opened just then. It was Wendy O'Connor, my colleague, office mate, and close friend. We never interrupted each other's classes, but there she was in the doorway, her elfin face ashen and her gray eyes wide. I made my way over to her, surprised when she motioned me to join her out in the hall.

Wendy was stone-faced. "Look. In today's paper." She pushed a copy of the *Jersey City Herald* so close to my face that I couldn't read it. "It says she was poisoned. Look. They did an autopsy. And the police think a student did it." Stunned, I reached for the glasses chained around my neck, perched them on my nose, and scanned the article. It was brief and only too clear. An autopsy had revealed that Dr. G had died of cyanide poisoning. I had to read the last line two or three times before its implications sunk in. "RECC student Oscar Beckman, nineteen, of Bayonne, is being held for questioning."

As if to reassure herself, Wendy, a resolute non-hugger, hugged me briefly before I reentered the classroom. The last time she hugged me was six years ago when she and I took Mark to the emergency room to have his head X-rayed and stitched up after a particularly nasty skateboarding accident. The hum of voices died away while the students, as always uncannily sensitive to the nuances of professorial mood changes, shifted in their seats and waited for me to speak. It was Rafik Haque who asked, "You okay, Professor?"

"No, I am not okay." I inhaled and continued, "I have just learned that, according to an autopsy, Dr. Garcia was poisoned." I pointed to the article in Wendy's paper that I still clutched in one hand. "And," I plunged on in spite of a few gasps and one whispered, but still highly audible "No shit" from the direction of Frank O'Leary, "the police are holding a student for questioning." I could hardly bear to say it, but I forced myself to add, "His name is Oscar Beckman."

I sat down and took a long gulp from my water bottle and then, in the stunned silence that greeted my words, I began slowly fanning my face with the folded newspaper. It was time to regroup. I heard myself say, "Let's come together in a circle now. What do you make of this dreadful news?"

A beeper chirped, insistent, intrusive, and infuriating. I'd just about had it with those damn contraptions. I tried to be modern, think nineties, but the beeper and cell phone factor had really altered the climate of our classroom, transforming it from a sort of sacred space to a kind of call-in hotline. The students couldn't escape for even a few hours from babysitters, kids, bosses, and Lord knows who else. College had not been like this in 1960. I saw Rowanda reach for her purse and check the offensive little gadget dinging away in there. Would she have to miss class time again to return the call? Last week she missed almost a third of the class to talk her son's baby-sitter through a teething-related crisis. I would have to schedule a conference with Rowanda to discuss limiting her beeper accessibility. I was relieved when this time she didn't immediately head for the hall to return the call.

Once we were all arranged in our familiar circle, Concepcion raised her hand. When I nodded at her, she spoke sharply, her voice rising steadily, "To poison her was just like killing Our Lord or Martin Luther King or anybody who tries to do some good. The good are always getting in the way of somebody who is bad. And people who are bad don't think twice about murdering someone in their way. It doesn't matter if you're a drug dealer or a college president."

Rafik's hand shot up as soon as Concepcion sat back in her chair, "But, Connie, she wasn't in no one's way. Dr. Garcia made this college better. She changed it from a vo-tech school to a real college. Now we can take a lot of liberal arts courses and transfer all our credits to a four-year school if we want. This is my fourth year here, and believe me, before she came, we had nothing. It's even because of her that we got accredited. Man, why would anybody want to kill her?"

Now it was Frank's turn. "Wouldn't you know they'd try to pin it on a student? Poor Beckman. He was in my English Comp class last semester. He's just another poor slob like me trying to get a piece of paper so he can get a decent job. The only thing he cares about is cooking. I practically wrote all his English papers for him, so you know what he did? He got me and my girlfriend two free meals each at that fancy restaurant he works at, De Trop, or something like that, out on River Road near Fort Lee. We went on Valentine's Day and for her birthday. I hope poor Beckman doesn't have to stay in jail long. He'll never last." I remembered that Frank was a criminal justice major, so I figured that's why he might have a more informed perspective on jail than the rest of us.

"Wait a minute. Oscar Beckman? I know him." Loritza, usually very reticent, looked surprised to hear herself speaking out. "I think he's the kid from RECC culinary school who volunteers on holidays at the shelter at my church. He makes turkey dinners and pies for Christmas and Easter. He has light hair and a lot of tattoos, right? A kinda medium build, not too tall? Only we call him Ozzie."

Rafik weighed in with, "I hope the college keeps on going and doesn't close because of this. It can't be too good for RECC's accreditation to have the president poisoned."

I didn't have time to dwell on the understatement that made Rafik's words almost laughable before Rowanda's hand went up tentatively. Looking suddenly older than her nineteen years, she asked, "Professor Barrett, do you know this Oscar Beckman? He ever in one of your classes?"

I nodded. "Yes. In fact, I had him in Speech last spring." I knew what was coming.

Rowanda pressed on, "So what you think? You think he did it? You think he poisoned her?"

I spoke directly to Rowanda's question, "I believe that a person is innocent until proven guilty. And no, Oscar Beckman certainly doesn't strike me as a murderer."

Now Rowanda didn't even wait for me to acknowledge her upheld hand before blurting out, "Why someone want to murder the president of this college? Where I live people be shooting and killing. But I come to RECC to get a better life for me and my son. Now they be murdering here too. I never thought nothing like this could happen in a college. I don't feel safe nowhere now, my son neither."

My stomach tightened as Rowanda's words registered there. On cue I began to sweat. Rowanda had articulated the unthinkable, and the unthinkable was real. There was a murderer, a poisoner yet, loose among us. Rowanda's fear was contagious. Automatically fanning myself with the newspaper I was still holding, I reflexively mouthed phrases that I hoped would assuage their fears. "This has been a terrible shock for us all, hasn't it? And as you were saying earlier, a great loss as well. But I'm sure that the police will find whoever did this, and that, in the meantime, the rest of us are not at risk. The Board of Trustees will appoint an acting president until they organize a search for a new president, so things should run smoothly. I'm sure RECC will not close or lose its accreditation." I tried to keep my voice steady, because, for the first time in over twenty-five years of teaching, I was lying to my students. I wasn't sure about anything now.

It was time for us to move on. Looking around at their serious faces, I said, "Take a few minutes so that those of you who wish may write a journal entry about Dr. Garcia. Perhaps we can use these to help us compose a letter of condolence to her family from all of us. Then let's turn our attention back to *Macbeth*."

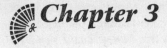 **Chapter 3**

October 20, 1994

Dear Professor Barrett,

I'm writing to you because my lawyer says I need character references from my profs to show the judge and jury that I'm really a good kid. I know you may not think I am one because when I was in your class I was not very polite to that lady who gave the speech on how where she comes from it's okay to mutilate females gentials or whatever, but I'm sorry. I don't go along with that. I didn't mean to hurt her feelings, but it seems crazy to have to sit in class and hear about stuff like that when all I really want to do is cook. Anyway, you were always fair to me and gave me an incomplete which was my highest grade in general education courses, so I figured I'd try you. All you can do is say no. Chef Lombard is going to write a letter for me and so are some of the other RECC chef-instructors. I may not be a good listener, but I didn't poison the president. If I was going to murder somebody, I wouldn't do it by spoiling good food. That's perverted.

The problem is the cops think I did it because after I was suspended last year I appealed the disapline committees decision and my case went to the dean and he sent it to the president and she ruled against me. When I found out, I was pretty mad at her, and I wrote her a pretty nasty letter about what she could do with her academic standards and all that. I told her she'd be sorry. I know now I shouldn't have written nothing down like that, but I was really mad. When the cops checked on all us culinary students who was at the festival, they found that letter in my file, so now they think I did it.

I don't want to make you feel sorry for me or anything, but my mom and dad are getting ready to put the deli up to bail me out. My mom is back in treatment over this and my dad don't look so good either. Even my stupid kid sister started wetting her bed again since I'm here and she's ten already. I try not to upset them by telling them what really goes on in here, but I hope I can hold out and that you will write the letter for me.

Your former speech student,
Ozzie (Oscar) Beckman

Believe me, my expectations for the memorial service were very low. I predicted that the tortured testimony of most of our local and RECC dodoheads would leave me dry-eyed, and I was right. The sad excuse for a tribute to our late president was a class A fiasco. Ostensibly organized by RECC's surviving administrators and trustees, the service was more likely the work of control freak Betty trying to organize Dr. G right into the grave. I was positive Betty was the one who actually reserved the auditorium, invited the bigwigs, printed the program, prepared the press releases, and ordered the two arrangements of amber mums. I hate to admit it, but Ramrod Ramsey (that's what Wendy and I call her) did a halfway decent job. Even so, the service just wasn't cathartic for me. I'll have to mourn Dr. G. on my own, but I did get through a lot of kegels while I was sitting there.

"... and forgive us our trespasses as we forgive those who trespass against us." Was Father Santos eyeing the trustees and other dignitaries beside him on the podium as he was intoning these words during the invocation? Looked that way to me, but what do I know? Next on the program was board president Tarantello extolling the virtues of acting interim president Nelson Danzig in the same breath that he extended condolences on behalf of the board to the Garcia family. Tacky, tacky, tacky. He called their loss a "most unfortunate event." Jesus. And even Commissioner Koladnar's silver tongue didn't keep him from sounding trite today. He talked about the "tragedy of her death." Blah, blah, blah.

While he droned on, I fumbled in my purse for my fan. As my hand closed around it, my thoughts drifted away from the rhetorical spin of the morning to the memory of my first hot flash, a watershed event that I actually enjoy thinking about sometimes. I was at a piano concert in Manhattan with Sol not long after we'd moved in together. Out of the blue, I broke out in a serious sweat. I sort of suspected what it was, so I fanned myself with my concert program during almost an entire Beethoven sonata. Sol saw my dripping face and just started fanning me with his program. We didn't talk about it after the concert because we were meeting some friends for a drink.

A few weeks later on the morning of my fiftieth birthday, when I opened my present from Sol, what did I find all wrapped in tissue paper? A fan. But not just any fan. No, it was an eighteenth-century French fan. It's the kind that was popular around the time of the Revolution, decorated with a simple picture of the fall of the Bastille. On the mounts there's a brief account of that event in French. I fluttered that exquisite fan all day right through the surprise party the kids had orchestrated. I even used it to help me blow out the fifty (count 'em) damn candles on my birthday cake. Of course, now I've got that fan insured, framed, and mounted on the wall, but I'm still sort of fan dependent. Today's is a gift from Rebecca that she found in Seattle's Chinatown. I grabbed it this morning because its purple and black design picked up the colors of my dress.

"Dr. Garcia was one of a kind, a college president whom we could look to as an example . . ." My reverie was interrupted by the unmistakable voice and clipped diction of Aruna Singh, president of the Student Government Organization, and one of my former speech students. "She came here for a better life. She studied and worked and raised a family just as we do. She learned a new language and a new culture. Like us she wanted to learn more. She walked where we walk today. She knew how hard our journey is because it had been her journey too." For the first time since the service began I heard people around me sniffle. Aruna's heartfelt words touched people in a way that the platitudes of the bureaucrats had not. I mentally patted myself on the back, recalling how tongue-tied Aruna had been just a year ago.

Representing the faculty was Academic Council president Harry Eldrich of the History Department. Harry recalled Dr. Garcia's fervent desire to infuse the "culture of RECC with the respect for scholarship and teaching excellence characteristic of the finest academic institutions so as to best serve the educational needs of our area's large and diverse population." Ho hum. He went on and on about Dr. Garcia's efforts to increase enrollment and her indefatigable lobbying for state funds with which to acquire a permanent waterfront campus. He reminded us that it had been Dr. Garcia who had rechristened Jersey City Technical College, dubbing it River Edge Community College in anticipation of the move. Finally, Harry voiced the faculty's devotion to her and extended our sympathy to the Garcia family. But even though Harry's words were unoriginal, he did manage to keep our attention because of his bizarre delivery. I guess he confused the occasion with a lecture because he kept pounding his fist on the lectern and gesticulating wildly. He looked like someone trying to arouse a roomful of sleeping students to the glory that was Rome instead of a mourner giving a eulogy.

There was, of course, the obligatory emissary from city hall speaking on behalf of the mayor's office about the importance of RECC to the area's high school graduates and others in need of higher education. The program told us what we already knew. The mayor himself was unable to attend because of "pressing commitments elsewhere," a polite way of saying that he was still serving time for fraud and embezzlement. It was getting really hard not to stick my finger down my throat.

Like Tarantello and Koladnar, the other speakers made only veiled references to the circumstances of Dr. Garcia's death; not a single one of them used the "M" word. In fact, Father Santos's sidelong glances were the only hints that Altagracia Garcia did not die of natural causes but at the hand of a murderer who had, indeed, trespassed.

After Father Santos's recitation of the Twenty-third Psalm, there was a moment of silent prayer, and then, thank goodness, the strange ceremony was finally over. I folded my fan and fled. A few rows behind where I had been sitting, I passed a small dark figure shaking with silent sobs. I was a little surprised to recognize Ramrod Ramsey. The sight of her hunched and heaving shoulders stayed with me as I rushed to my office. I didn't want to be late for my appointment with one Illuminada Gutierrez, a new adjunct in Criminal Justice. Jawad Mamoud, her coordinator, had suggested that she contact me for some mentoring. She was a private investigator with no prior teaching experience. Since she sounded pretty desparate on the phone, I'd agreed to get together with her.

I was not expecting anyone else, but waiting outside my office, swaddled in a bright blue and green sari, stood Rheka Patel looking a little like a gift someone had wrapped and left at the door. Only a few months gone from her village in the Punjab, Rheka was in my Introductory ESL class. She stopped by frequently for translations, reassurance, and mostly, I think, to practice her English. I ushered her into the office.

As usual, the tiny cubicle was crowded with two desks and chairs, overflowing bookcases, and piles of papers. Wendy and I have been pushing each other's stuff out of the way in there for years. The heaps of students' journals and essays beckoned, a weekend's worth of work. I really wanted to get started on it this afternoon, but no, I had an appointment with that damn adjunct.

"Rheka, how are you? Did you go to the memorial service for Dr. Garcia?"

"No." Rheka sat at Wendy's desk, her books stacked on her lap. "I did not know about service. I am sad by what happened to the president of this college. This my first semester here, and I not expecting death. Why they could not save her? Did they not have good medicine in the United States?" Before I could reply, Rheka went on, her books teetering as her words stumbled out, "My uncle, he not know that she ate poison from a student. I trow out the paper even if he do not read English good. If he find out, maybe he tink I not safe in the class at RECC. He maybe say I have to withdraw from this college." I struggled to recall what she had told me of her uncle and aunt, who had sent for her to help care for their kids in return for the chance to get an education. Would her uncle really make her withdraw from college now? She was blossoming, becoming more fluent every day.

I barely got out the words, "Oh Rheka, I hope not," before she was off again.

"Sanjay's family want me to marry with Sanjay. His wife dead last year with cancer. He have one kid. Now his mother she take care with the kid, but she very old. He come from my village and his whole family live here now. His family business good. They have spoke with my uncle."

"Oh my goodness, do you like Sanjay?" was the best I could do by way of response to this news before Rheka resumed her monologue.

"I do not wish marry with Sanjay, take care with his kid and his old mother. She is not nice woman." Rheka's words came more slowly now, and the books settled once more in the center of her lap. She looked directly at me as she formulated her next pronouncement, "I want to be American accountant lady. I have to stay at RECC and finish my studies or marry with Sanjay. I hope nothing stop me from finishing my studies, even this poison death."

"Oh Rheka, I'm sure you'll finish your studies. You're such a good student. You learn so quickly and you study so hard." I guess I said the right thing because Rheka rewarded my words with a lovely smile as she left my office for her next class.

 *Chapter 4*

To: Menopausesupportgroup@powersurge.com
Subject: Yoga
Date: Fri, 21 Oct 1994, 02:03:30
From: Bbarrett@circle.com

Thanks for the encouragement about exercise. I especially like the idea of doing yoga when I can't sleep. You're right. I haven't been making any time for fitness lately. And it's kind of relaxing to stretch when no one else is up. The phone doesn't ring and the house is quiet. I feel almost glad now when I wake up at some ungodly hour because I have something better to do than just lie there sweating and worrying.

In fact, these nocturnal yoga sessions are the only serene intervals in my life now. It's been established that the president of my college was poisoned. The whole place is in an uproar. Students are scared and worried that the school might close. The faculty are sad and a little scared too. Even the administration seems more shell-shocked than usual. I can't believe that the student being accused is, in fact, guilty. RECC has always been a stressful workplace, and now it's worse.

I was desperately hoping the Gutierrez woman wouldn't show up. I mean, why is it always good old

31

Bel who gets stuck mentoring every wannabe professor who adjuncts at RECC? This was the third time this semester I had to try to distill twenty-five years of teaching knowhow into a nutshell for some young twit who probably has no classroom experience and even less motivation. Sol's right. I should "just say no." I mean, would somebody go into court to plead a case without first going to law school? Or try to perform brain surgery without going to medical school? I don't think so. But everybody and his uncle seems to think they can teach without any preparation. It's infuriating. This is exactly the kind of thing I was going to pull back from, do less of, refuse altogether. The last adjunct I spent so much time with didn't even thank me. And that reading teacher I worked with at the beginning of the semester, the one who always dresses entirely in green, never returned the books I lent her.

I heard a knock. Damn. She wasn't going to stand me up. As I threw open the door, I saw a petite black-haired woman wearing a trench coat and sneakers and carrying a briefcase and a shoulder bag. Offering her hand, she announced, "Illuminada Gutierriez."

"Bel Barrett. Delighted to meet you." My smile was dazzling, Oscar-worthy. "I'd offer you a seat, but it's so claustrophobic in here. Let's take a walk. I'll give you a tour of some of our buildings, and then we can stop somewhere for coffee." God, I was gushing over this person I didn't even want to know.

"Sounds very good to me. It'll be good to stretch my legs after that service. You see, I'm ready to walk." Illuminada pointed to her sneakers.

"Leave your briefcase here. We can stop back later and get it, and then I'll give you some sample syllabi and a few articles you might want to look at." I was still into my Miss Manners mode as we left.

"Great. I really appreciate your taking the time out to do this. Especially with all the upheaval." I noticed the program from the memorial service protruding from her shoulder bag.

I was impressed that at least she was polite, and even more important, she knew what was going on here. She had actually been to the memorial service. So many adjuncts just run in, teach their class, and run out to their next class or job somewhere else. We have some who don't even know when our exams are scheduled. But who can blame them for not taking the place too seriously? They're exploited beyond belief. RECC pays adjuncts less than other area colleges, and no colleges pay adjuncts well. But I'm not getting started on this because I get too wound up.

So anyway, I said to Illuminada, "'Upheaval' is putting it mildly. I still can't believe that Dr. Garcia is dead, let alone that somebody poisoned her. But I suppose you run into this sort of thing all the time in your work?"

"Not exactly." Illuminada looked up at me as she explained, "I spend most of my time doing computer searches following paper trails left by runaway fathers. When that proves unproductive, I drive around asking ordinary people some very routine questions. Boring." She simulated a yawn for emphasis. "That's one of the reasons I decided to teach part-time."

"Oh. And what are the other reasons?" I posed this question as we strolled through the Friday afternoon frenzy of shoppers and commuters toward the RECC Culinary Arts Building a few blocks away.

"When my daughter was old enough to go to school, I decided to go back for my degree, and I went to community college in Texas. We were living down there while my husband was in the service. I was so nervous and worried about would I make it, would I be the dumbest one in the class, would I be able to write a paper or pass a test. *Dios mio*, I was a basket case. But Raoul, he's my husband, he really pushed me. He knew how much I wanted to get my degree even though I was afraid. Anyway, community college was great. The teachers were very supportive, and I turned out to be pretty smart." Again Illuminada looked up at me, this time with an unmistakable twinkle in her eye, before going on. "I finished my two years and transferred to the university for my bachelor's degree. Then I was really scared because I figured that I might not have the background to compete at the U."

"And did you?" I knew the answer, but I wanted to hear how this young woman would describe her success.

"*Caramba!* Yes." She grinned up at me now. "I had studied hard while most of my younger classmates were drinking beer and looking for love. I graduated magna cum laude in two more years. So, now that my daughter Luz is in college, corny as it sounds, I decided to give something back. And this place pays so little that I feel I really am donating my time. But I want to do a good job."

"I'm sure you will." I wasn't sure. Not at all. It takes a lot more than good intentions to teach. "How do you like teaching?"

Illuminada paused before replying slowly, "It's very interesting, but not quite what I expected. I lecture and explain, and then last week I gave a test, and hardly anybody passed." Her voice lowered and she sounded genuinely disappointed.

"What kind of test?"

"You know, an essay test on some of the history of the criminal justice system. We've been reading about it, and I've been lecturing on it for weeks. But so many of them have problems writing and, for that matter, reading, and others had not studied or, worse, they had studied badly somehow. I felt terrible when I read some of their papers."

I felt the adrenaline rush I always get when I have the chance to sound off about teaching nontraditional students such as she had once been. Right there on the busy sidewalk I couldn't resist launching into what turned out to be a half-hour monologue on learning English as a second language/dialect. Illuminada was actually taking down every word I said on some sort of pocket computer she typed on with only her thumbs. I paused for breath, annoyed with myself for having slipped so effortlessly into my role of mentor. We resumed walking. I was relieved that Illuminada had pocketed her tiny machine.

We reached the gray fieldstone structure that houses the RECC Culinary Arts Institute. I really like this building. It's a three-hundred-year-old former farmhouse, which stands out amid the neon and grit of the rest of the area. Before the surrounding neighborhood deteriorated and RECC leased the building, it had been an upscale steak house. Now students attend class there in shifts and cycles. They prepare breakfast, lunch, and dinner for themselves and their instructors in the large restaurant kitchen and serve these gourmet meals in the dining room. The second-floor rooms that once were bedrooms of the farmer and his family are now seminar rooms, and below street level the rabbit warren of cubbyholes that had been the root cellar currently houses faculty offices and a tiny lounge. Students' lockers line the basement walls. Even though the adjacent field has been a parking lot for most of a century, the building still has a faint aura of coziness and charm. It's the nicest building we have.

"Home of the pride of RECC, our answer to the Cordon Bleu. They have no classes on Fridays so the students can do their internships, but I'm sure the offices are open. Want to look around?" I was surprised at my geniality. When had I stopped doing Illuminada a favor and started warming up to her?

"No, that's okay. I'm enjoying the air and the walk. Let's keep going."

But I stopped walking and stood in front of the farmhouse. I heard my voice say, "You know, the boy that the police think poisoned Dr. Garcia is a Culinary Arts major."

"What's he like?" Bless her, she sounded really curious.

"He's absolutely obsessed with cooking. I had him in Speech last year. He's a funny kid. I mean, he has a kind of quirky sense of humor." Before Illuminada could respond, I blurted, "He reminds me a lot of my son Mark."

"Do you think he did it?" Illuminada's question caught me off balance. I've had literally thousands of conversations with colleagues about students during the twenty-five years I've been teaching. I'm used to discussing students' performance, motivation, and needs, but I've never conversed about whether a student has murdered someone. Even so I was encouraged by Illuminada's curiosity and impressed by her ability to chat almost casually about a topic that I myself was still having trouble even conceptualizing, so I went on, "I really can't see Oscar Beckman killing anybody. Frankly, Oscar can be really rude, and he is sort of single-minded . . . But I know he wouldn't kill anybody."

"What do you mean 'rude'?"

"Oh, he's kind of hostile toward anything he's not interested in. He's very single-minded about cooking, but he has to take general education courses like English, speech, and psychology to get his associate's degree. During other people's speeches, Oscar would sometimes put his head down and just look bored. Once during a speech by an African woman, he rolled his eyes and made rude remarks under his breath, but we could all hear them. I finally had to speak to him."

"What on earth did you say?" Illuminada was clearly interested in the nuts and bolts of classroom management.

"I reminded him that in Speech students are graded on listening, and that if he expected to pass, he would have to sit up and tune in. Then he got suspended, so he missed the rest of the semester. I was half relieved to lose him."

"Half?" Damn. I was struck again by how many questions this woman was asking. She wanted to know everything. Meanwhile I was struggling to ignore an idea forming in my mind.

"Well, he wasn't a bad speaker as long as he could talk about what interested him. He was clear and informative. And his speeches *were* getting better." I spoke kind of distractedly because I was still trying to resist the new notion, now fully formed, and the familiar urge I get to fix things.

"Why was he suspended?"

"I heard that he was caught cheating on an exam. I assume that's why." I sighed, resigned once again to losing the battle between my urge to make things better and my common sense. As a high school fresh-

man in the fifties, I had carried my first placard pro-
testing the fact that Passaic High had never had a
female student government president. Ever since
then, I've been championing underdogs. My ex-
husband Lenny decided to leave me when I spent our
fifteenth wedding anniversary chained to a giant red-
wood tree in California instead of in bed with him in
a B&B in the Amish country. But that's another story.

Illuminada was nodding and then shifted the subject slightly by asking, "I suppose there were lots of
people who didn't like Dr. Garcia, weren't there? She
couldn't possibly have been in Jersey City for two
years and made all those changes I read about in the
newspapers without gaining some enemies." By now
I was starting to feel a little like I was being grilled,
and I remembered Illuminada's day job. She must be
relentless in pursuit of those deadbeat dads. They
didn't stand a chance. What an ally she would be! I
sensed my inkling hardening into resolve and my
common sense retreating into that part of my head
reserved for New Year's resolutions and diet plans.

"Oh God. You are so right. She had enemies. She
was very independent. She fired people, she held national searches for new people, she expected faculty
and staff to work hard, to put the students first. And
she said what she thought. I mean, sometimes she
could be very charming, but she could also be sharp,
sarcastic. If she were a man, they'd have said she was
'no nonsense' or 'hard-nosed,' but she was a woman,
and a foreign woman at that, so she was 'bitchy.' 'The
Dragon Lady' they called her. But not the faculty. We
loved her. She was like our guardian angel. Before she
came, no one listened to us. I just can't believe that
she's been poisoned." My own voice was low now.
Recovering a bit, I looked up and, remembering my

role as tour guide, remarked, "Here's our former Student Activities Center."

"*Caramba!* This?" asked Illuminada. Her voice was shrill with disbelief as she took in the crumbling faux flagstone facade and the fading RECC sign dangling menacingly from the eaves.

"Yes. When Dr. G came, she refused to allow students to use this old flophouse. Inside it smells of stale beer and cigarettes." I stuck my index finger into my mouth and made a gross gagging sound just in case she wasn't getting the picture. "It's not even up to code. This dump was what actually inspired her to try to get state funding for a waterfront campus."

Illuminada looked at her watch. Responding to her gesture, I said, "You're right, it's time for coffee. There's a diner around the corner where faculty and students often go."

"You mean the RIP? I like that place. It hasn't changed in years." That was an understatement. At the RIP, decaf is Sanka, tea is Lipton, and milk is whole. No one could ever accuse the RIP of being trendy.

We entered and seated ourselves in a corner booth. I ordered a cup of hot water into which I dropped an herbal tea bag from a stash in my purse, and Illuminada ordered black coffee. I looked straight at her across the table and made my move. In the special voice that I use to cajole potential drop-outs to stay in school, speech-phobic students to address the class, and blocked writers to compose research papers, I said, "Illuminada, I just know Oscar Beckman didn't kill Dr. G. And the more I think about her being murdered, the more I want to figure out who really did do it and why. And now here you are, a bona fide private eye sitting right across the table from me. I just have to ask. Will you help me?"

"You mean pro bono?" Illuminada screwed her delicate features into a grimace. "I do this sort of thing for a living. But . . ." she grinned as I whipped out my fan and began to circulate the air around my face, "for the mother of all mentors. To vindicate our shared heritage, mine and Dr. G's," she added hastily as it was my turn to look quizzical, "and finally, because if we do unravel this, it'll be good for business. I'll make a deal. If you let me observe a few of your classes, I'll do a little poking around." Laughing, Illuminada raised her coffee cup in a toast and then we awkwardly clinked cups, sealing our compact.

Still fanning, I said, "I'm going to find out everything I can on my own. Then we'll know where to look further."

"You better be careful, Professor. Like it or not, somebody did poison Dr. Garcia and that somebody is not going to appreciate your curiosity. This is not exactly library research." When had this role reversal happened? Now who was mentoring whom?

I responded to her warning with more confidence than I felt. "Oh, I'm just going to chat up people the way I always do. One of the advantages of being the faculty yenta-in-residence is that people are used to me having my nose in everybody's business. No one takes me very seriously. I'll start with Betty Ramsey. She was very close to Dr. Garcia. She'll help us. Don't worry about me."

 *Chapter 5*

To: Menopausesupportgroup@powersurge.com
Subject: Hormone Replacement Therapy
Date: Fri, 21 Oct 1994 16:50:16
From: Bbarrett@circle.com

In response to those of you who suggested that I look into HRT,
my mother has had two mastectomies, so I'm probably not a
good candidate for hormones, but I guess it can't hurt to talk to
another doctor. I'll give it some thought, even though it's pretty
scary to think about. Again, thanks for writing back.

P.S. Maybe my newfound calm in the midst of chaos is the result
of one of those infamous menopausal mood swings rather than
the yoga? What have you all experienced?

P.P.S. Be careful, Hallie, with that vitamin E. Too much isn't
good for you. I forget exactly why, but you can look it up. It's
in Gayle Sand's book.

As soon as I got home, I listened to the answering
machine. "Bel, Wendy. We're not going away, so
weather permitting, let's walk on Sunday. Usual time

41

and place. Your turn to bring the binoculars."

"Mark to Ma Bel. Sorry, but I'll be about an hour late picking you up for dinner. Look for me just after eight, okay? I have to work late."

I kicked off my shoes. God, I was glad to have a few minutes to recover from the bizarre goings-on at RECC. What with morning meetings, the surreal memorial service, Rheka's whirlwind visit, and then my conversation with Illuminada Gutierrez, I hadn't had a second to relax and, after all, it was Friday. TGIF! All I felt like doing right then was pouring myself a glass of sherry and curling up on the loveseat. I just wanted to snuggle in with my cuddly black cat Virginia Woolf and wait for Mark without thinking about anything to do with work. I popped in a Scarlatti CD. Holding my glass of sherry in one hand and stroking Virginia Woolf's soft coat with the other, I melted into the cushions. The cliched speeches and my meeting with Illuminada replayed themselves in my head like scenes from a half-forgotten film, not really anything to do with me and my humdrum life. It was lovely to be home, quite removed from both poisoners and private investigators.

My thoughts turned to Sol, away on another long business trip, this time to Eastern Europe. Sooner or later he'd phone. Then I'd decide how much of this business about Dr. G to tell him. At first he'd be incredulous and then horrified. Sol's not like Lenny, my ex-husband, though. Lenny's main objection to my social conscience was that it inconvenienced him when I was too busy or preoccupied to whip up the perfect dinner for twenty or slip into a naughty-looking nightie for a little hanky-panky. Sol's different. He has a do-gooder agenda of his own. In fact, we met at a party thrown by the Citizens' Committee to Preserve the Waterfront to celebrate victory over the mayor's first proposal for high-rise waterfront development here in Hoboken.

We had won a referendum by a margin of only fourteen votes, and I was, as my daughter would say, "really psyched," not to mention a little drunk. Singing "We Have Overcome," a group of us ambled over to Erie Lackawana Plaza overlooking the Hudson. Ever since Hoboken's hot bar scene became a magnet for suburban singles, the police have gotten used to packs of noisy drunks roaming the streets at all hours, so they didn't bother our motley crew. Gradually people drifted off, leaving Sol and me alone to contemplate the view, which we felt we personally had rescued from the forces of evil. The two of us stood there talking for hours and then went to Schaeffer's, an all-night coffee shop that used to be around the corner, and talked some more. And we've been talking ever since.

When we finally decided to live together in what we describe as "domestic partnership," neither of us wanted to leave Hoboken, so Sol moved in with me, bringing, of course, his computer and his baby grand, his "boy toys," I call them. I decorated Rebecca's old room for guests and for the occasional crashing kid temporarily out of a job, a relationship, or an apartment. In warm weather, I love reading in the tiny garden. What a treat to have a private oasis spitting distance from work and, of course, from Manhattan. And to top it all off, both Sol and I had indulged in the luxury of pricey parking spaces in a vacant lot on the corner. Let me tell you, parking in Hoboken is a blood sport. There's nothing like trekking home from some far-flung parking place to take the edge off an evening out.

But Sol is a worrier. He worries about me if I'm ten minutes late or cough twice on the same day. He makes me take calcium, and he's actually the one who found me the on-line menopause support group. I didn't want to push his worry button by telling him there had been a murder at RECC, let alone that I was looking into it. And I *would* be fine. Nobody'd even notice me poking around since I'm always into everybody's stuff. Anyway, women my age are invisible.

I felt myself starting to mellow. I looked around at my collection of miniature china shoes, piles of books, and the stack of students' papers on the floor next to the loveseat. Even though our snug two-story flat in Hoboken is only a few minutes from RECC, the atmosphere here on lower Park Street, a block of nineteenth-century brick-front row houses, harks back to a more peaceful and ordered world.

Actually, the halcyon days of early Hoboken are one of my favorite sherry-induced fantasies. In reality, downtown Hoboken grew out from the railroad terminal and the harbor, and around 1850 when our block of houses was probably built, nearby First Street was becoming the Mile Square City's commercial heart. There would have been the hustle and bustle of the marketplace, not to mention the throngs of tourists and sailors spilling out of the theaters and bars along River Street.

I was getting almost too relaxed to pour myself another glass of sherry, but finally I reached over my feet for the bottle on the floor. Every single day at RECC, I struggle to understand the cultural, linguistic, class, and generational perspectives through which my students and my colleagues view the world. Cultural pluralism is exhausting! I think that's why I find it incredibly restorative to return each night to *my* books, *my* music, *my* shoe collection, and, sometimes, *my* sherry. It's especially cozy when Sol and one or two of our kids are around, but to tell the truth, after relating to so many different people all day, I really relish time alone too. And I've always got Virginia Woolf for company.

I planned to spend all day Saturday, as usual, reading and responding to student papers. I've grown to savor reading students' work unless I've had one of those weeks from hell. Reading my students' essays and journals and commenting on them is a little like having a hundred or so pen pals. I love being privy to the ideas, feelings, and stories of so many people, all with such brave dreams, such American dreams, *the* American dream. Altagracia Garcia had tried to help them fulfill those dreams, and now she was dead. Sitting there, my defenses weakened by fatigue and sherry and the comfort of home, I felt the tragedy and injustice of Dr. G's death sink into my soul. So when Mark finally honked outside, the sound interrupted the cathartic interlude I had promised myself earlier in the day. I wiped away tears of rage and sorrow before I put on my coat and went out to join him.

"Sorry I kept you waiting, Ma Bel, but the Grants were late getting home again. I couldn't leave my precious charges alone. They might kill each other." Mark looked a little down. At twenty-two he's working as a caregiver for a family with two kids on Boulevard East in Weehawken. Nannying had started out as summer work, but he'd stayed after his exhaustive search for an entry-level position in publishing or public relations had failed to turn up a single full-time job offer. He loved the kids though, and Josh and Jared loved their burly, bearded nanny right back. Most evenings Mark rather halfheartedly pursued a graduate degree in Teaching English as a Second Language at NYU. Periodically he threatened to go to Israel and join a kibbutz.

"What's all this stuff in the paper about RECC? So this time they're not indicting the president, but murdering her?" Unfortunately Mark read all the bad press RECC got before Dr. G. came, and so he harbors no illusions about the college. In fact, he can't understand my affection for the place. He was off and running. "Give me a break. Is this the same woman who came to your annual open house last New Year's? The kick-ass one who said I ought to play professionally?" In fact, Dr. G *had* come to our annual open house and *had* praised Mark's guitar playing.

"Yes, but if you don't mind, I'm rather sick of talking about it. It's awful really. Tell me about your week." I opened my fan and peered over it at Mark. I was trying to look curious without appearing to pry.

"All right, but you better give everybody an A. We don't want some crazed RECC student slipping something in your sherry."

"Mark," I snapped. And, as he has since babyhood, Mark totally ignored the warning in my tone.

"Well, I'm worried about you. Remember that dude who said you should be shot because you recommended him for counseling? And the guy who kept making those anti-Semitic remarks? And the woman who wanted a strand of your hair so she could put some kind of curse on you? I'm glad they've got this kid in custody."

Had Mark always been like this, or had he patterned his excessive concern for me after Sol's? Come to think of it, Mark was the same kid who came home from school one day and flushed my Salem Lights down the toilet after somebody from Smokeenders had brought in a blackened lung to show his class. That gesture had effectively ended my career as a smoker. Or is his current concern, like his cynicism, an aftermath of the divorce and Lenny's too quick remarriage? Maybe, just maybe, Mark's overprotectiveness is a reflection of my own? After all, he *had* been the only kid on the block whose mother made him wear a helmet when he played bottle caps.

At any rate, I decided not to mention to Mark that the alleged perpetrator was about to be released on bail or that I was planning to chat with him very soon after that. Nor did I allude to the information I expected to extract from Betty Ramsey during my dinner date with her Sunday night. Instead I refocused the conversaton.

"So how's work? And how are your classes?" Now he could take his pick of topic and tell me about whichever part of his life he deemed, at the moment, most appropriate for Mom.

"Actually, they both suck. I love the kids, but Charles has been downsized. Can you believe that? They're keeping him on until Christmas, and then he's out." Mark took one hand off the steering wheel and made an abrupt chopping motion meant to convey the finality of Charles Grant's expulsion from corporate America. "He's been with the same company for eight years, and they axe him?" The questioning inflection revealed Mark's shock at this injustice and, I suspect, his sense of the futility of his own attempts to find other work.

"Now after Christmas they won't be needing a nanny. So I guess I'll finish this semester at school, and then who knows? Maybe a kibbutz or sliming in the Alaskan fish canneries. I sent for a Peace Corps application. I'll go wherever they'll pay me and put me up." Mark spoke defiantly now, with that edge to his voice which stifled my arguments and left me momentarily mute. I pictured my son's body shattered by a zealot's homemade bomb in the Middle East, his severed hand bloodying salmon canning machinery in Alaska, his fever-wracked form writhing on the floor of a Senegalese hut.

When I did speak, I said only, "I'm so sorry to hear about Charles. It's good that Diane has her work to tide them over until Charles gets a new job. And I'm glad that you have such interesting plans. It's always wise to have options." Then I literally placed my tongue between my upper and lower front teeth and kept it there for three kegels in order to obey the mantra of all mothers of Gen-X children: "Keep your mouth shut." When archeologists of the future exhume and examine our bodies, they'll wonder why so many middle-aged women have ridges of scar tissue on their tongues. The mothers of adult children among them will, no doubt, figure it out. After this conversation with Mark, talking with people at work about Dr. G's murder should be duck soup.

# Chapter 6

To: Rbarrett@UWash.edu
Subject: More Red Hot Mama
Date: Sat, 22 Oct 1994 22:16:24
From: Bbarrett@circle.com

Dear Rebecca,

Maybe a line or three to you will calm me down. I guess it's normal to be sort of agitated when the president of your college is poisoned. You're right, only at RECC could this happen. I mean, until Dr. G's death, my semester was just more of the usual, too many students, too little time, and, for that matter, space. I may collapse from exhaustion (only kidding), but God knows, I'm never bored here.

On top of everything else, I'm still adjusting to my spiffy new trifocals (black with round frames, I wanted the Gloria Steinem look, but these are actually more Bella Abzug). Before much longer, I should be able to tell who's raising her hand and who's just scratching her head or stretching.

I don't see what's the big deal about me joining an on-line menopause support group. You're getting very conservative since you left Hoboken. Could it be something in the beer out there? Anyway, several of us have complained about having had no preparation for menopause at home or in school. (Is it covered in that Anatomy and Physiology course you're taking?)

Remember when you were little and I used to get you all those books about ovaries, eggs, and pubic hair? There was one that described the uterus sloughing off its lining every month and you didn't know what "sloughing" meant, remember? Do you realize that those books all ended with birth? Well, this is the sequel! The story's not over till the fat lady sweats! At least you aren't going to be one of those "my mother never told me" women.

I was so unprepared I stopped menstruating before I began to deal with the idea of stopping, if you can follow that. I guess I didn't want to face it. I was a little anxious about growing older. I still am. But I won't start wearing makeup or coloring my hair. I mean, what you see is still what you get. It's just that what you get is an older grayer mère than she used to be! (Sorry, Becca, I couldn't resist.)

I'm relieved that you were able to coordinate your hours at the restaurant with your classes. Give my love to Keith. How does he like telemarketing? Any chance of you two coming home during your December break?

Love,
Mom

P.S. I'm sorry your car was towed again, but that's why I gave you that credit card, for emergencies.

It wasn't hard for me to get up early Sunday morning to walk with Wendy at Liberty State Park. I just love that place. This would be the first time I'd been there since Dr. G's death, but no way was I about to let morbid thoughts spoil the park for me. Wendy and I always meet at the same spot, a bench not far from the snack bar where the walkway curves around to span the bay. From there you can practically pat the backside of the Statue of Liberty. Ellis Island is to the left, framed by the sunlit spires of lower Manhattan. Not exactly a bad place to hang around waiting for someone, right?

"BINOCULARS!" The word glared at me from the lavender Post-it on the dashboard of my car. Remind me to buy stock in Post-its if I ever have any extra cash. I don't know how people managed before some genius, probably a memory-challenged genius at that, invented them. Thanks to that little purple piece of paper, I actually remembered to take the binoculars from the glove compartment and slip their strap around my neck. I locked the car and headed for our bench.

Except for a jogger vanishing around the bend, I had the park to myself. From the path alongside the empty parking lot you see a quintessentially New Jersey vista. Directly across Newark Bay is Caven Point, a gritty working shipyard. Closer in is Port Liberté, an island community of luxury housing designed to look like a cross between Camelot and a Venetian palazzo. Built in the real estate boom of the eighties, Port Liberté went belly up a few years ago and floats there now, less than half occupied, like a ghostly theme park. When its developer went bankrupt, Dr. G, visionary that she was, tried to convince the mayor that Jersey City should buy Port Liberté to use as a campus for RECC. It would have been a dream campus.

Suddenly over the picnic area I spotted a large low-flying bird, black against the browning leaves of a sycamore tree. Raising the binoculars, I tried to focus on the dark blur. Was it a duck or a cormorant? Just then from somewhere behind me something big and fast slammed into me. My whole left side exploded with pain and my legs caved in. Lying flat on the macadam, I was too winded and scared to yell. It wouldn't have mattered if I had though because there was no one to hear. By the time I looked up, the Rollerblader who'd knocked me down was a far-off flash disappearing behind the building that houses the snack bar and rest rooms.

For seconds I just lay there. Then after a few breaths, I sat up tentatively, testing each bone and joint. Thank God for those calcium supplements because nothing felt broken, even my left wrist, which had taken a lot of my weight. The left side of my rib cage ached, but I didn't feel the stabbing pain that, I figured, would indicate a fractured rib. My neck had been jerked back by the field glasses when they flew out of my hand on impact. Their strap had snapped them back so that when I went down, they landed on my head. I would have a goose egg on my noggin and a bruise on my side, but I would live.

I was relieved to see Wendy approaching from the direction of the bicycle rack near the refreshment stand where she had locked her bike. Shaky and sweating, I stood up. I knew I was feeling better because I was starting to get mad at the kid who hadn't even stopped to see if I was okay. How would he like someone to do his mom like that? Wendy's greeting interrupted my internal tirade, "What the hell's the matter? Did you trip? You look awful." Wendy's never been one to mince words.

Rubbing my neck and handing her the binoculars, I sputtered, "Some crazy Rollerblader knocked me down and didn't even stop. Must have been going fifty miles an hour. Scared me to death. It's a miracle I didn't break something." I began rubbing my wrist.

Wendy looked at me. "Are you okay?" When I nodded, she went on. "I passed a serious blader on my way in. He was moving right along, even wearing a helmet and goggles. I figured that's probably why he was here early, wanted to speed train or something. We'll report him when we pass the Environmental Center. Not that it'll do any good. Did you get a look at him?"

I answered with feigned indignation. "Obviously not. I thought I saw a cormorant, so I was focusing the glasses. Besides, he came up behind me. I didn't even hear him. By the time I could look up he was on the other side of the snack bar."

"Well, Audubon, let's walk. It'll do you good to move or you'll stiffen up. It'll take a day or two for bruises to show, and then I'll give you more sympathy. We'll start slowly. Come on, I'm dying to get your reaction to Lord Nelson's latest memo. Is that guy crazy, or what?"

"I don't know if I saw it. I never got back to the office to check my mailbox on Friday."

"I think I have it." Wendy reached around and pulled a crumpled piece of RECC stationery out of her fanny pack. "Get this, 'In these troubled times, it is imperative to assure students that the sturdy vessel that is RECC will sail through these rough waters as we have sailed through storms in the past.' He's into his Horatio Hornblower persona."

Contemplating the nautical nonsense of RECC's newly appointed acting interim president always convulsed us. Wendy and I kept a file of especially memorable RECC memos, and Nelson Danzig had authored more than his fair share. "So go on, what else?"

Wendy tried to make her voice nasal and whiny

like Danzig's, but it was really the man's words that got me as she continued to read, " 'Furthermore, during my watch as acting interim president and captain of our ship, I will do everything in my power to ensure the safe passage of our troops, our students. Faculty and staff can improve morale below deck by working hard and remembering that the name and reputation of the good ship RECC are in the hands of our trusty and talented crew.' "

In spite of the ache in my side, it felt good to giggle. When my giggle became a guffaw, I felt even better. Danzig's words were providing me with laugh therapy, the best kind. The man was a real upper. Finally I was laughing so hard I had to swipe at my eyes with a Kleenex. "God, that man is too much! Finish it, go on."

"He actually says Dr. G received a 'send-off worthy of a good seaman,' " Wendy was laughing so hard herself that she was having trouble reading. She barely managed to deliver the memo's finale, " 'Finally, in preparation for the annual visit of the accreditors this winter, let me remind you that it is not too early to plug the leaks, stock the galley, and swab the decks. When we welcome them aboard, everything must be shipshape.' "

My response came out as half snort, half hoot. "Jesus, he really is crazy. Isn't it ridiculous? Dr. G was planning to replace him, I'm sure. There was going to be a national search for an experienced veep who could reorganize our bookkeeping, budgeting, and facilities management. Now she's dead, and he's president."

"Yeah, and according to yesterday's paper, the board gave him a $15,000 raise when they appointed him."

We had resumed walking. "What a surprise. So now he's making $85,000 a year or something like that, right?" My question was rhetorical, my voice harsh with contempt. "What other monkey business did our untrustworthy trustees enact?"

"Not much, but they did announce that we got the grant Dr. G had been working on. We now have a million bucks from the state to do the needs assessment and the site search. You remember, those are the first phase of her campaign to develop a waterfront campus."

"She sure would have been happy about that. Dr. G really hated the fact that we had to use crummy rented facilities while so many other community colleges in New Jersey have gorgeous campuses they built in the seventies. She hated paying those outrageous rents for the leased buildings too."

Wendy sounded resigned when she added, "Yeah, well, the trustees renewed all the leases at the same special meeting. In fact, it was a unanimous decision."

"Dr. G would be horrified—Danzig appointed acting president, the leases renewed, the grant coming now. My God, she must be turning over in her grave." The cliche was out of my mouth before I could stop it. For once Wendy didn't jump on me.

Instead she said, "You know, I don't think it's really hit me yet. That she's dead, I mean." Then in a lighter tone, Wendy asked, "Wasn't that service something else? Did you catch Tarantello? The fat guy with his foot in his mouth? He outdid himself. God, what a crew."

"Wendy, did you ever have Oscar Beckman in one of your classes?"

"Yes, he took Children's Literature last semester as an elective. He was doing pretty badly, cutting classes and not doing the reading. But he'd started work on a children's cookbook for his term project. He'd actually done a draft including some fairly classy drawings. It's kind of charming. I didn't tell him, but I entered it in a contest. If it wins, he'll have a shot at getting it published. I can see him sculpting Garcia nude in meringue, but I can't see him poisoning her."

"Me either. In fact, I'm trying to figure out who might have. One of the new adjuncts, a private investigator, said she'd help me. Any ideas?" Wendy looked thoughtful, but when she didn't respond, I went on. "You know, I wrote Oscar a character reference. Why don't you write one too and tell about the drawings and the cookbook?"

Wendy nodded. Then she looked up and quipped, "If you're going to play detective, you'd better rethink your fashion statement." She looked me up and down, taking in my faded blue windbreaker and baggy gray sweats. She shook her head, indicating disapproval. As usual Wendy herself looked like she had just stepped out of an L. L. Bean catalogue.

We stopped at the Environmental Center to report the hit-and-run Rollerblader and continued talking and walking, enjoying the nearly perfect autumn day. By the time we had circled the park, I felt relaxed, ready for brunch and the Sunday paper.

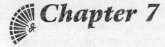 Chapter 7

To: Menopausesupportgroup@powersurge.com
Subject: Coping with Symptoms
Date: Sun, 23 Oct 1994 12:16:17
From: Bbarrett@circle.com

This menopause mailing list is a lifesaver! Thank God Sol found it for me! And thanks for the tip about lecithin as an antidote for a menopausal memory. I'll try it. If I remember :=). I hope it works because the memory loss really bothers me. I used to learn the names of all my students in a few days. Now it takes longer. Much longer. And sometimes I go to get something from my bookcase or from my desk and forget what I'm looking for. If I don't write things down . . . Now what was I saying?

But there's an upside. I'm finally learning how to refuse when people ask me to take on more responsibilities. I've always picked up the slack for others at work and at home, and now, sometimes, I just say no. It's really hard, but this semester I refused to head the damn Sunshine Committee for our department again. Let someone else mail the get well cards and order the food for the Christmas party for a change. And I've programmed the number of our neighborhood Thai take-out restaurant into the phone at home. If this isn't wisdom, what is?

Neither my bruised body nor my aching head kept me from meeting Betty Ramsey for dinner at the Sechuan Village Sunday night. Betty had sounded surprised to hear from me, but she was amenable to getting together. Of course, she chose our meeting place, midway between Hoboken and her home near Route 440 on the other side of Jersey City.

A relative newcomer to Jersey City and to RECC, Betty had been one of Dr. G's first hires. But sorry to say, even though Betty had brought order to Dr. G's office, the board meetings, and the busy president's hectic schedule, few of us on the RECC faculty could stand her. Although she had worked well with her dynamic and idealistic boss, the obsession to control that drove Betty's efficiency had apparently blinded her to the feelings and needs of others lower in RECC's hierarchy. Ramrod Ramsey had earned her nickname.

Barely seconds after the waiter had put the menus on the table, Betty announced, "We won't be able to finish two main courses, so we'll split one and have two appetizers. The shrimp dumplings are especially good here and the scallion pancakes too. I really liked the eggplant with garlic last time I had it. You'll love it. And, of course, brown rice, okay?" Biting my tongue, I put aside further thoughts of the succulent spare ribs and sweet chunks of General Tso's chicken I had been mentally savoring on my way to meet Betty. I was relieved that she didn't protest when I asked the waiter to bring us two Ching Tao beers.

"Where did Dr. G find you?" I queried after Betty ordered our dinners. "One minute there was total chaos and the next moment there you were. Wendy thinks you arrived like Mary Poppins." I was being as pleasant as possible in spite of my companion's need to decide where and even what I ate.

"Well, you're not far off. Father Santos is the connection. He knew I needed work, and he knew Altagracia needed an assistant, so he got us together, and the rest is history." A rueful smile flitted across Betty's face.

"So you both went to St. Paul's?"

"Yes, but we never would have run into each other. We usually went to different Masses."

"I know how close you two were. This has to be very hard for you." I remembered Betty sobbing at the memorial service and felt a pang of compassion for the woman across the table even though she had the social style of a sadistic drill sergeant.

"Yes. Javier invited Father Santos and me to the house. I'm the only one from the college who was invited. He explained to me why the family wouldn't have the funeral service here. They shipped her back to El Salvador. Understandably, they're very bitter about what happened." Betty's eyes were down and her head lowered during most of this conversation. I had to lean across the table to catch her next words. "They didn't want her to be buried here."

Maybe that was why Betty had invested so much energy in the memorial service. Arranging it had been the last chance she would have to work for Dr. G. "I can't blame them. How're they doing?"

"Her husband still seems shocked, you know. Like he can't digest it. He's drinking a lot, I think. Javier's a very passionate guy, a painter. Altagracia used to joke about what a romantic wild man he was. She once was kidding around and said he was the salsa on her taco." Again Betty smiled at the memory. Then she went on, "But I'm more worried about the boy." Betty's jaw tightened. "Andreas is fourteen. That's a tough age. They get depressed." She squared her shoulders and looked up at me. Her voice was stronger, intense. "Next week I'm going to look into finding some sort of bereavement group for him, you know, a group for kids who've lost someone."

Damn, the woman even wanted to manage the family's grief. She's just such an organizer, absolutely obsessive. But nobody had controlled Altagracia Garcia. And for a kid Andreas's age, joining a bereavement group was probably an excellent idea. I decided maybe I should give Betty the benefit of the doubt. Besides, the beer and dumplings had come, and they both tasted pretty good. I reached across the table and touched her hand. "And you? How is Betty Ramsey doing?"

At my touch Betty began speaking in choppy bursts. "I detest being in that office without her. I hate working for Lord Nelson." She stopped and looked me in the eye. "The whole place has begun to smell . . ." Betty paused. She continued to look directly at me, adding sharply, "There are a lot of people who are actually glad she's gone."

"You don't think Oscar Beckman did it, do you?"

Betty frowned, and then, still looking straight at me, said, "No. I most certainly do not. I can name at least three others who stood to benefit directly from her death, and, if I look through the files, I can come up with a few more."

Damn. Beads of sweat slid from my hairline down my back and shoulders. I got out my fan and steeled myself. "Betty, I'm trying to find out who really killed her."

Betty blinked as if I'd surprised her. She shot back, "And just how do *you* expect to do that?"

With great effort, I ignored the challenge implicit in

the way she dragged out the word *you*. The way she drawled out that pronoun made it clear that in her opinion the noun it stood for, Bel Barrett, was too ditzy to live let alone to investigate a murder. *I love you too, sweetie,* I thought.

What I said, though, was, "Not without your help." At first I couldn't tell how she was taking my not-so-veiled invitation. At least she hadn't left the table.

"Tell me more." Betty was looking right at me, waiting.

I spelled out what I was making up as I went along. "Well, for starters, helping means telling me whom you suspect and why," I paused briefly to acknowledge her nod. Good, she was still with me. I continued, "And you are in a position to Xerox all her papers and go over the copies with me."

This time she nodded and spoke, "Yes. I could do that." On a roll, I added, "And since you were, literally, by her side when she died, I'd like to hear your version of exactly what happened that night."

This time when she nodded, her eyes filled up and I felt another twinge of pity for her. But she hadn't committed herself yet, so I went on, "There's a private investigator who's going to help too."

"Who?" Betty's monosyllabic query might have covered some relief that we would have a professional ally on our side.

"An adjunct in Criminal Justice. Illuminada Guttierez. She agreed to work with us. So please think about it. Let me know in a day or two."

Betty looked up, about to speak. Then, as if she had suddenly thought better of it, she nodded and lowered her head once more. Suddenly she snapped her head back up, squared her shoulders again, and said, "I don't need a day or two. I just thought about it.

Count me in. And I'll get you those files. I'll just stay late a few nights and copy everything. Look for a package to be delivered to your home by courier service later this week."

I couldn't believe how easy it had been to enlist her cooperation. And now she was going to get us the files. It was too good to be true. I was so relieved I only cringed a little when she continued, "After you've gone over everything I send you, the three of us should get together at my house. Here's my address." She made a swift foray into her purse, pulled out a business card, and handed it to me. "Take Route 440 to Bayview Estates, which is just past Pathmark on the right. I'll leave your name with the guard at the gate, so he'll let you in and direct you to my condo. How does Friday night at seven sound to you?"

I recognized a rhetorical question when I heard one, but I was still so pleased to have Betty's help that I didn't argue with her. Besides, if she wanted to play hostess, that was okay by me. The new Bel Barrett was out of the hospitality business for good. I smiled my assent, clicked shut my fan, and picked up my chopsticks, saying, "And now tell me, don't you have a boy starting college? Randy, right? How's he doing so far? Does he like his roommate?"

 **Chapter 8**

October 25, 1994
Dear Professor Barrett,

Thanks for the nice letter and for sending it so fast. My
mom and dad and my sister say to thank you too. I will be
glad to meet with you whenever you want. I got nothing
but time since as you probably seen in the paper, I'm out
on bail (my folks had to put up the deli to post it) but I
can't work with food. It's a condition of my release. That
means I can't go back to the restaurant. (The lady who
owns it is really okay. She wrote a letter for me too. And
so did the nun in the shelter where I sometimes help out.
But I won't go near the restaurant or the shelter till this
is over. No one is going to pay $75 for a meal that they
think might be poisoned. I can't even cook for the homeless
now.) The worst thing is I can't help my folks in the deli,
and even though they ain't said nothing, I know business
is way off. And of course, I can't go to school because I was
taking garde manger and pastry and table service this semester, and they are all hands-on courses. But I got to go
over there to clean out my locker, so we could meet there.

How about around three on Friday when there are no

classes? I don't really feel like running into anyone from school, if you know what I mean. If that's not good, my phone number is 555-9204.

Ozzie Beckman

By the end of the week, I found myself full of resentment about Betty's attitude. She made our Friday night meeting seem like a command performance. Again I couldn't help but wonder what the hell was wrong with that woman. I still couldn't get past what a martinet she was. I knew I should have been grateful for the two cartons of files she'd sent, but God, it was the week before midterms, and as yet I had not had even a few minutes to look at them. In fact, I wanted to postpone our get-together for another week, so I could really study those records. But I was afraid some sort of edge would be lost if we let too much time go by. After all, as Illuminada said, this wasn't library research. I hated to admit it, but Betty was probably right to want to move things along. The thought of her being right was pretty annoying too. I couldn't win.

If only it hadn't been the week before midterms. It's such a hectic time. Every spare moment was scheduled with conferences about papers and speeches. Conferencing has always been a special interest of mine. Often I tape these sessions so I can see how I might improve them. I'm glad I taped my session with Frank O'Leary the other day. He was clearly hostile when he arrived. I could tell by the way he stormed into my office, wedged himself into Wendy's chair, accordion-pleated his legs, and fired his opening salvo, "I don't get it. Why do we have to make up the questions for our midterm? Why can't you just use the same midterms as last semester like everybody else does and get it over with? This is so much bullshit. I'm sorry, but I just took my chemistry exam, and it was the midterm from hell. Anyway, you make us do so much writing already, I don't see why we have to have some stupid exam. You make us write journals and reader responses and papers. I have so many conferences with you, my girlfriend's getting suspicious. If you don't know how I'm doing by now, well, I don't want to say it." I thought he might be pausing for air, but Frank just kept on talking, his voice dripping with sarcasm, "And don't tell me you want to prepare us for taking other exams in our academic futures, 'cause everybody else gives multiple-choice exams or true and false or whatever. If I have to take a midterm in this class, I will, but I'll be damned if I'm going to make up the questions."

"Well, Frank, why don't you tell me how you really feel?" I looked up at him, suspecting that he had just a little more venting to do before we could get down to the real business of the conference, which was determining a paper topic.

Frank grinned. "Sorry if I sound a little hostile, but this day has been a bummer from the start. There's construction going on over the pharmacy, you know, where I work, and I have to really sweat to keep the floor and stock halfway clean. Actually, it's not so bad now. It was really gross when they first started building 'cause I kept finding dead rats out back by the trash. Ever pick up a dead rat?"

"Can't say that I have, but it doesn't sound like much fun."

Frank looked more relaxed now that he had unloaded his troubles. His tone was noticeably lighter. "Speaking of fun, you picked the perfect play for Halloween. Ghosts and everything. My girlfriend read *Macbeth* in high school, and we were thinking of going to her cousin's Halloween party as Lady Macbeth and Banquo's ghost. Terri was going to smear her hands with red food coloring and wear a long nightgown. I was going to wear the traditional sheet. But we were afraid nobody would know who we were dressed as, so now we're going as Tonya Harding and her ex-husband. She'll wear her skating gear and I'll carry a billy club and look dumb. That's the hard part." Frank grinned all out, and I had to smile.

Encouraged, he continued, "Seriously, I am into the play big time. I hope we can read a scene or two aloud. I really like the part where Macbeth sees the ghost. Isn't it amazing how guilt gets to some people?" I nodded, and Frank went on, "My totally favorite lines so far are in the scene where Macbeth describes to Macduff finding Duncan's body and killing the guards. This part is totally awesome. He is so full of it. He says all that stuff about Duncan's 'silver skin laced with his golden blood' and how Duncan's wounds looked like a 'breach in nature.' I always admire somebody who can throw the bull, especially under pressure."

"I can see how you might appreciate that ability, Frank," I interjected archly. "You too have been intimate with the Blarney Stone. Seriously, I'm very glad you're engaged by the play. Not everyone is, you know."

"Yeah, it was tough at first, but I cracked the code when we heard the tape, and I'm reading faster now, getting used to the old language, I guess. But I still don't know what to write my paper on. Any suggestions?"

It didn't take me long to get Frank interested in

writing a paper comparing Shakespeare's treatment of guilt in *Macbeth* with Woody Allen's ruminations on guilt in *Crimes and Misdemeanors*. All in all it was a pretty useful conference, but just one of five I had that afternoon. The flurry of midterm conferences reminded me that I was scheduled to present on conferencing at a national convention in November, and I should have been preparing for that too. My workload seemed overwhelming. Reading those files might just be the straw that would break this camel's aching back.

After my Friday classes and four more conferences, I dragged myself over to the RECC Culinary Arts Institute. The gray clouds above matched my mood. I just hoped the rain would hold off until I got home. Entering the building, I noted that the security guard was nowhere in sight. He was probably having a smoke in the parking lot. I remember how Dr. G had equipped RECC's archaic and arthritic security force with beepers and hand-held phones and mandated training sessions for them. Most of the brigade of geezers entrusted with protecting us had friends or relatives on the Board of Trustees or in the mayor's office, and so they were genuinely shocked by Dr. G's mandate that they actually patrol the buildings and monitor comings and goings. It sure hadn't taken long for the "old guard" to revert to their old tricks.

I made my way down the dimly lit stone stairwell. After a few feet, I realized that I had no clue where in the maze of corridors Oscar Beckman's locker was, so I took a guess and turned right down a narrow passageway. There was no sign of Oscar. Suddenly I froze. There was absolutely no logical reason for the paralyzing terror I felt. I knew full well that no hairy professor-eating ogre lurked in the Culinary Arts

Building's basement. And no burglars would venture there either, for there was little to steal. But I didn't need real ogres and burglars to push my flight-or-fight button. Not anymore. Of late I panicked for no reason whatsoever. And so, there in the dark cellar, I resigned myself to the onset of a full-fledged anxiety attack. Sure enough, I could hear my heart pounding. Sweat broke out all over my body, first a film, then a flood. My hands and feet started to feel numb, so I tried flexing my fingers and wiggling my toes. Suddenly I felt a slight pressure on my shoulder. I jerked upward so hard that my head hit the low ceiling, and I collapsed, dazed, on the slightly slimy stone floor.

"Goddamn!! Professor Barrett! I'm sorry. I didn't mean to scare you. You're lookin' for me, right? You okay? Here, lemme help you." A very flustered Oscar Beckman extended his hand awkwardly and I grasped it and heaved myself up, adjusting my sweaty blouse and smoothing my skirt as best I could. I was getting pretty good at hauling myself up off the ground lately.

"I'm sorry I jumped, Oscar. I don't know what's the matter with me. I'm fine now, really. Thank you." And, damn it if I wasn't suddenly just fine. The numbness had retreated from my fingers and toes, my heartbeat was no longer audible, and the sweat that had covered me like a second skin just a minute before was evaporating. Except for yet another bump on my head and a slightly disoriented sensation, I felt quite myself. Maybe these occasional moments of panic were yet another message from my body to my brain, a warning to slow down and sample the fudge. I resolved to see what the support group had to say about anxiety attacks.

I followed Oscar to his nearby locker, which he was

surprised to find empty. "I guess they wanted to use it for someone else." Squaring his shoulders, he continued, "Maybe my adviser, Chef Lindstrom, has my stuff. I'll call him Monday." Eager to leave the damp cellar, I suggested that we head for the RIP.

As soon as we were seated in a booth, Oscar lit a cigarette. I asked our waitress for some ice wrapped in a napkin to hold against my throbbing head. Once Oscar's coffee and the hot water for my tea arrived, I wasted no time introducing the topic I'd come to discuss. "Oscar, exactly what happened that night at the festival? You were right there. I mean, what really happened? Tell me everything you remember."

Oscar knotted his brow and looked, sometimes at me and sometimes at his stubby fingers with their chewed-down nails. He tried to blow the smoke from his cigarette away from me as he answered. "She was comin' down all the aisles, tastin' the food, talkin' to everybody. Everybody was followin' her. That black lady and the trustees . . . I don't know all their names . . . and the senator and Dean Danzig. They was all eatin' too. Everybody had a plate. When they would get done with one aisle, they would bunch up in a little group for a few minutes 'n' talk 'n' laugh and keep eatin'. I guess so their plates wouldn't be so full for the next aisle."

"Did you notice if they shared the food from their plates?"

"Gee. I'm sorry. I didn't watch that close. I did notice that it was between aisles when they would sometimes get somethin' to drink. They were all fallin' all over themselves tryin' to get her some punch."

"Oh really? And did you notice who did get her punch?"

Oscar's voice lowered as he replied, "No. Gee. I'm

really sorry. I was busy servin' it. I didn't look that close."

"Oscar, this is all very helpful. Don't worry about what you didn't see. Let's concentrate on what you did see. What else do you remember?" My temperature began to rise, and the ice I was holding against my head melted faster. I was literally losing my cool. I put down the now sopping napkin and got out my fan so I could deflect the smoke from Oscar's cigarette while he spoke.

"When they started down my aisle, she was laughin', and she stopped at every dish and said how good it was. She spoke in Spanish too. I don't know what she said though." Oscar looked crestfallen as if his inability to understand Spanish were evidence of yet another failure on his part. "I guess you was right. I'm not such a great listener, am I?"

"Oscar, please go on."

"Then she kind of choked and got all red and fell. She dropped her food and everythin'. Seemed like she was havin' some kind of fit. The black lady started screamin'."

"And then? What happened next?"

"Well, the board guys and another guy, the commissioner I think it was, and Lord . . . I mean Dean Danzig, they was trying to push people back so she could breathe, I guess. They got really excited. They was knockin' over the food even and shovin' the tables. All of 'em knocked into me before it was over. I was tryin' to get close to see if maybe I could do a Heimlich maneuver like that guy gave a speech about in our class, remember? So I guess I was in the way. I could see they didn't mean nothin'. They was just tryin' to make room."

"I know the paramedics came then and took her to

the hospital. What did you all do next?"

"We cleaned up, you know. People were leavin' in a hurry. The party was definitely over. The bands left. And since the college ain't insured to give leftovers to a shelter where they could use 'em, we had to throw all that stuff out. There was tons of good food left, and we had to dump it all. It was a crime." Mercifully oblivious to the irony of his comment, Oscar shook his head at the memory of the wasted food. "After we bagged all the trash, we went back to school to put all our gear away, you know, our knives and our uniforms and all the serving stuff." As Oscar came to the end of his story, outside the first drops of rain began to fall.

 *Chapter 9*

To: Menopausesupportgroup@powersurge.com
Subject: Hot Flashes
Date: Fri, 28 Oct 1994 07:40:16
From: Bbarrett@circle.com

Trudy, you are so right. If I stop fighting the hot flashes, they end sooner and aren't quite so extreme. Now I just mop myself up and try to keep my mind on whatever else I'm doing. My students are getting used to me dripping and fanning away at the blackboard. In one class when I sweated right through my blouse in several places, I just told them that I was menopausal, and so from time to time I become very warm. Some women nodded knowingly, a few blushed, and one or two of the guys also looked embarrassed. But nobody passed out or had any kind of overreaction. They're too worried about their own midterms to get very unhinged over my midlife. Come to think of it, I can remember gushing milk all over the place when I was nursing Rebecca and Mark. But I guess that was different. Was it?

I seem to be coping better lately. My friend Wendy says it's because I have more testosterone and that's making me more assertive and stronger. Do you think that's true? Has anyone else experienced that?

When I got home, a quick shower, fresh clothes, and an apple and Swiss cheese omelette went a long way toward eradicating the terrifying sensations of the afternoon. I was soothed by the familiar presence of a hungry Virginia Woolf slinking around my calves. After I fed her, I checked my answering machine. There was a message from Sol. How would I like to spend the Christmas holidays in Azerbaijan? He was revelling in his new role as visiting guru consulting to several entrepreneurs starting businesses there. He missed me. Even my disappointment in Oscar's story, bereft as it appeared to be of new or useful information, faded. Maybe Illuminada or even Betty would be able to glean something from it.

So a little later, I set out for our meeting at Betty's house. I crossed over Kennedy Boulevard and was headed down the ramp toward routes 1 and 9 where they feed into the Tonnele Avenue circle. The Friday evening traffic was thinning as I braked for the stop sign. Suddenly my whole body tensed. Something was wrong. The pressure of my foot failed to slow the car. I floored the pedal, but nothing happened. Damn. On the rain-slicked decline, my car was actually picking up speed. The car in front of me was just a few feet away, getting closer every second. I jerked the emergency brake, and for a moment my whole car convulsed in place. Then it hurtled forward into the vehicle ahead and shuddered to a stop.

I sat there for a minute, amazed that I was still alive. No one had been immediately behind me, thank God. I undid my seat belt, surprised that my hands were steady enough to manipulate the buckle, and got out of the car. The man whose car I had plowed into was also getting out. He was scowling. Was he going to make a scene? He was so young, so nattily dressed. Would he sue? Would my insurance go up? Like me, he had no passengers. Thank you again, God. He did, however, have a cellular phone, and he was using it. I figured he was probably calling his lawyer or his insurance company. I hoped he'd also call 911. I reached back into my car and switched on my hazard lights. They'd be small comfort to drivers in the line of cars already forming behind me. Even though my aging Toyota's front end was accordion-pleated, the warning lights blinked on. The rear end of the sleek new-looking black sedan I had hit was similarly reconfigured.

I put out my hand. "Bel Barrett. So sorry. I lost my brakes."

"Ron Swenson." He ignored my hand. There was no absolving small talk, no comforting "Don't worry about it. That's why we have insurance. Thank goodness no one was hurt."

A little hostile, but who could blame him, I thought, pulling my hand back. "I'll give you my insurance info." I started fumbling in my purse.

"I called 911. The police are on the way."

"May I please borrow your phone?" Wordlessly he handed it over. I dialed Triple A and then Betty's house.

"Be sure to get his insurance info," barked Betty. "Are you a member of Triple A? Have you phoned them?"

Damn. She must think she's talking to a teenager, I fumed silently.

While waiting for the police, Ron and I exchanged insurance information. Occasionally one of us flexed an ankle or rubbed a shoulder, checking for pain or stiffness. There was no conversation. Ron looked at his watch every minute or two. I did kegels. By the time the police and the tow trucks arrived, Illuminada and Betty were pulling up too. Before much longer the ramp was cleared of glass and debris, my car was towed, and Ron Swenson and I had gone our separate ways.

I was actually glad when we pulled into Bayview Estates where the guard at the turreted gate had acknowledged Betty, kind of as if she were a queen returning to her castle, and waved us through. I'd often been critical of what I'd always thought of as the paranoid elitism inherent in gated communities. But that night I reacted differently. The sight of the uniformed guard in his electronically fortified kiosk, the orderly rows of townhouses, each with a lawn of bright green sod, and the well-lit jogging path along the perimeter of the wall surrounding the compound were reassuring symbols of safety and order in a chaotic world. I could see why many retired cops chose to live there.

We settled quickly into Betty's living room, a loft-like space decorated with large abstract paintings, like those in an upscale doctor's waiting room. After making the obligatory call to my insurance company's answering service to report the accident, I was trying to relax on Betty's leather sofa with my stocking feet extended on a killim-covered hassock. Illuminada sat cross-legged on the floor opposite me, and Betty hovered tense and upright on the arm of a big leather chair.

"Feeling better now?" Illuminada asked.

"No, not really." Illuminada's face fell when I answered, but she leaned forward as I continued. Betty raised her eyebrows and looked at me as if to ask, "Now what?"

"What I didn't mention to the police is that my car just had a complete brake job last week. It was in the shop for two days. I mean, those brakes were brand new. I spent over $500 on them. And they worked fine until tonight."

"What are you saying, Bel?" As Betty asked the question, she poured each of us a little Chivas. I prefer sherry or wine, but I didn't feel like making an issue of it.

"What I'm saying is that I think someone tampered with my brakes while I was home, just before I came here. My car was parked for about an hour and a half across the street in the tiny lot where I always keep it. It was dark. Somebody could have gone in and quickly done whatever he had to do to ruin the brakes."

"Just take out the pin under the dash. Shouldn't take too long. Did you notice a puddle? Oh. I forgot about the rain this afternoon." As usual Illuminada had a question. She even had the answer.

"No. I didn't think to look. Oh God. I sound just like Oscar Beckman." I filled the others in on Oscar's version of Dr. G's last moments. Betty was taking down every word on her laptop. After I finished speaking, they fell silent, mulling over what I'd said, and how it fit in with what each of them already knew.

Of course, Betty spoke first. "I hate to admit it, especially since I was right there with Altagracia, but I don't remember much more than Beckman. There was so much going on. She still had her talk to give. There had been a problem with the sound system. Nobody knew for sure whether the governor was going to show up. I just wasn't watching what that girl ate."

Betty grimaced at what she clearly perceived as gross negligence on her part. Illuminada reached out and stroked Betty's arm saying, "Of course not. You were keeping track of everything else."

In contrast to Illuminada's gentle gesture and soothing tone, my next words sounded stern. "Betty, this murder isn't your fault. Don't blame yourself because you didn't anticipate that some psycho was going to poison your boss. You were an executive assistant to a community college president, not a Secret Service bodyguard."

Illuminada looked up. "I guess you two don't know that when they searched his locker, the cops found an empty vial containing traces of lead cyanide in Oscar Beckman's uniform pocket."

That sure got our attention, and Betty snapped, "How on earth did you find that out? It certainly hasn't been in the paper."

"A few years ago I did some lost and found work for a clerk in Homicide, and Faith is pretty grateful. So on a hunch, I stopped by late today and asked her what they had on Beckman since Bel's so sure he didn't do it. A few juvenile offenses on his record, his suspension, that threatening letter he wrote, and the cyanide vial are pretty strong evidence against him. The cops are busy, and now that they've got the method, the motive, and the opportunity, they aren't even questioning anybody else." Illuminada delivered this fusillade of information in a matter-of-fact tone.

"Oh God. I remember when Altagracia read that letter." Betty was smiling for the first time all evening. Transformed by a memory, she stopped typing. "When she showed it to me, we both broke up. We just assumed he was going to do a nude ice sculpture

of her like that other one he did. We had a running
joke about how far off the ground her boobs would
be and what he would do with her butt. That girl was
blessed with a very small butt. We kept waiting for
an X-rated masterpiece to pop up in some really embarrassing location. She never took his threat as anything very serious, though. She figured the dude was
just letting off steam."

"Well, to Homicide it's a motive. As far as they're
concerned, Beckman poisoned her. Open and shut.
They're not even working on it anymore. Motive,
method, and opportunity. They think Beckman had
them all. And there's something else. This case didn't
come in as a homicide. So the scene of the crime, what
they would normally go over first, was cleaned up.
Faith said everything was thrown out, mopped up,
and washed away long before Homicide was even involved. She said they were lucky to get Beckman's
uniform."

This was all pretty discouraging, so I suggested we
order a pizza. Betty looked hurt and disappeared into
her kitchen. When she returned seconds later, she was
carrying a tray of smoked turkey, brie, sliced pears,
and breadsticks. I settled. In between mouthfuls I
said, "Tomorrow when I talk to Greg, my mechanic,
about my car, I'll see what he can tell me about why
the brakes died tonight. Oscar Beckman may have
been mad at Dr. G, but he isn't mad at me, and I think
somebody messed with my brakes. Do you think I'm
being paranoid?"

Illuminada was the first to reply, "No. I think
you're being smart. I hope you'll also be very careful.
Do you have any idea why anybody would try to hurt
or frighten you? Who knows you're involving yourself in this?"

Betty stiffened and when she spoke, her words were clipped. "Nobody, I hope. None of us should be discussing this with anybody." For a brief moment I pictured myself shaking her. Where did she get off telling me who I can and cannot talk to?

"Oh, just Wendy and Oscar Beckman. Wendy and I have been friends since our twenty-something children met making mud pies in a sandbox in the park. We share an office. When she wants more space, she just shoves my stuff over. She doesn't try to kill me." I gave Betty a look, daring her to defy me. "And Oscar . . . well, he knows I'm on his side."

I guess Betty accepted my explanation because she changed the subject in her most peremptory manner, saying, "When should we three meet again? We should decide now." As usual it was hard to argue when Betty was in gear. Did she know how much she sounded like one of the witches in *Macbeth*?

I was snickering to myself over this when Illuminada offered, "Next Friday night? Let's get together at my house. I'll e-mail you both directions. And when I observe Bel's class Tuesday morning, I'll collect the files. You'll have finished with them by then, right, Bel?"

I nodded, even though I knew reading those damn files would replace reading my beloved Sunday papers.

"And I'll go over them as fast as I can after that, so by Friday we'll all have done our assigned reading, okay?" Illuuminada stood up and pushed away her empty plate. "*Dios mio*, it's late. Come on, Bel. I'll drop you off. Thanks so much for having us here, Betty."

Chapter 10

To: Menopausesupportgroup@powersurge.com
Subject: HRT
Date: Sat, 29 Oct 1994 03:00:00
From: Bbarrett@circle.com

It's amazing to me that so many of you wrote to say that I should look into HRT in spite of my mother's history. You've actually persuaded me to get a second opinion. I've been going to the same guy for over ten years. Now I'm asking around about a different gyno in my area.

I mean, my doctor's very nice, but when I try to talk to him about my anxiety attacks (and did I have a doozy of an anxiety attack yesterday!) or mood swings or insomnia, he says stuff like, "There's a lot going on in there." Once he popped his head up from between the stirrups and told me I was "winding down nicely." I had such heavy bleeding for five years that I wore only black or navy skirts over super tampons and a super humongous maxipad. At night I slept on two towels over a rubber sheet. What was "nice" about that?

Sometimes I think my doctor doesn't know a whole lot about menopause. I realize there's not as much research as there should be, but he's not the type to say, "I don't know" either.

He doesn't even seem comfortable talking about menopause. I'll keep you posted on my search for a new doctor. I have enough on my plate now without having panic attacks, insomnia, and short-term memory loss. Damn. I didn't realize how angry I was until I wrote all this.

I ran faster. He was gaining on me. Looking over my shoulder, I could see him gliding silently, effortlessly closer to me. I took great gulps of air as my jog became a desperate sprint, but when I looked back again, he was bearing down on me. And then he was right behind me, so close I could feel his breath on my neck, his weight pushing me down. I could feel his elbow crashing into my ribs, crushing my ribs . . .

I sat bolt upright in bed, tangled in sweaty sheets, my left arm outstretched, wrist bent, as if to cushion my fall. As the nightmare receded, it left a message that was clear even to me, the original denial queen. I suddenly understood that the Rollerblader who'd run me down at Liberty State Park last week had done so deliberately in order to hurt and frighten me. He'd not only skated into me, but he'd made sure I fell by elbowing me in the ribs. Of course he hadn't stopped to help me up. And now I knew with equal certainty that someone, maybe even the same fiendish Rollerblader, had also tampered with the brakes on my car. Reaching for Virginia Woolf, I pulled her warm body close and lingered a few extra minutes in bed, reliving my two narrow escapes. Perhaps like the purring black cat kneading my chest, I had nine lives. I hoped so.

Later that morning, Greg, my former student and longtime mechanic, confirmed my sense that someone surely wished me ill or worse. Greg was talking to me in the patient tone he always used. "Yeah, Professor, what happened was, like, somebody broke into your car, probably to steal it." Although I didn't say a word, I wondered if I had even remembered to lock my car. I sometimes don't, but I've been lucky. It's a big bone of contention between Sol and me. "Then all he'd have to do is reach under the dashboard and pull the pin. The brakes would die pretty soon after that. You got some student you gave an F to?" Greg saw that I wasn't laughing, so he said, "Seriously, you know that gizmo Sol rigged on the ignition to, like, prevent the car from being jump-started by a thief? Well, my guess is that some guy was trying to, like, steal the car and couldn't start it, so he got pissed, you know, and, like, pulled the pin." Greg looked pleased with his explanation. I didn't argue with him. The notion of someone sneaking behind the shrubbery and into our tiny parking lot, breaking into my car, and setting a potentially lethal trap for me was just too scary to dwell on.

So I left it alone and spent the day responding to papers and preparing midterm exams. Maybe Frank O'Leary was right when he said I shouldn't ask students to create essay questions and topics for their own exams. It sure was a lot of work to wade through their suggestions, but I know it helps them to see what's important in their courses and makes them more active learners. They sure do resist it though. Rheka was particularly opposed to the idea. She wrote, "You the teacher. Why you not know what to put on exam? In my country the teacher make up exam." But she came up with two excellent suggestions anyway, so I felt that my approach was validated.

In the evening, with Virginia Woolf curled contentedly in my basket of unread *New Yorkers*, I worked on my upcoming presentation. It was only a few weeks away. I played tapes of conferences I'd had with students and planned how to use them. By bed-time, I was exhausted, but my mind was filled with the stories of my students and excitement about my presentation.

Because I still had no car that Sunday morning, Wendy drove us both to Liberty State Park. Even though I was determined not to be spooked by what had happened, I was really glad not to be in the park alone. "You know, Wendy, the brakes on my car died Friday night on my way to Betty's."

Wendy looked annoyed. "Excuse me, but didn't you just get new ones? When are you going to ditch Greg and go to a real mechanic? What does it take?"

I replied slowly, "It's not Greg. It's that somebody tampered with them so they would give out almost as soon as I got on the road. Somebody broke into my car in the lot across the street and pulled the pin. It's under the dash. Greg actually explained to me how it's done."

Now Wendy sounded incredulous. "Why not just steal your car? That's what happens to the rest of us." She's bitter because she's had two cars stolen in the last three years.

"Wendy, remember the Rollerblader who knocked me down last week?" I stopped walking. "Well, I think he did that on purpose to scare me, and I also think somebody deliberately messed with the brakes on my car so I'd have an accident. Somebody wants to stop me from trying to clear Oscar Beckman. Do you think anybody knows I'm involved in this mess?"

Wendy started walking again, "Of course people know you're poking your nose into things. After all, you did write that letter for Oscar. And you had coffee with him at the RIP, for God's sake. Bel, you know perfectly well how RECC is. Marco, the security guard at CAI, saw you leave there last Friday with Beckman. And he told Carlos, the new maintenance guy in the Administration Building. He and Gloria—you remember Gloria who used to be our clerk-typist?—well, she now works in the mailroom. Anyway, Carlos and Gloria are an item at the moment, so that means that our very own Hilda got it when she placed her Mary Kay order with Gloria, and Hilda told me Wednesday.

"Bel, you know only too well that the most informed people at RECC have always been maintenance, security, and clerical. If they don't know it, it's not worth knowing. And, believe me, people know you're up to something. You better be careful. You're not exactly inconspicuous, you know."

"Are you making nasties about my designer clothes again?" I flashed open my electric blue ruana, revealing jeans and an old T-shirt of Sol's tie-dyed into concentric circles of bright red and yellow.

"Yikes. In that museum piece you even look like a target." Wendy couldn't help giggling. Then she reverted to our favorite pastime, griping about work. "I can't believe I've been tapped for another search committee. Why me? Don't I have enough to do?"

I knew my lines, and responded accordingly, "Well, better you than me. I was on three last year. Who are we searching for this time?"

"Danzig says we have to hurry up and hire a director for the Career Development Center." Wendy sounded resigned.

"Wendy, we don't even have a Career Development Center yet. Dr. G was trying to get the corporate community to fund that position anyway," I interjected. "Are we doing a national search?"

"Bel, how long have you worked here? Sure, we're doing our own version of a national search. Here's how it goes. Danzig says we have to 'weigh anchor and set sail ASAP' and to help us, he and a couple of board members have personally screened the hundred or so résumés that came in from all over the country and selected a candidate to interview." Wendy's voice dripped with scorn.

"Have you seen the résumé?" I asked.

"Yes, and the interview's tomorrow. The résumé is definitely worth saving for the files. I have a copy in the office, but I remember a few highlights."

"Such as?"

"Well, the candidate has previous experience working as a sewage maintenance and efficiency laborer. He put the acronym SMEL right on his résumé in caps. It's easy to remember," Wendy was once again on the verge of a giggle.

"What else?" Somehow, I knew there would be more.

"He's also worked as a debris management officer, which I think translates as a garbage man. And you know who his boss was?"

"Let me guess. His dad."

"Close. His uncle, at Tarantello Brothers Container Company. We have here a little Tarantello." Wendy extended her thumb and index finger to underscore "little."

"So let me get this straight. The nephew of the president of our Board of Trustees, an experienced Dumpster emptier, is applying for the position of director of Career Development? What garbage."

"Not as bad as that joke. Why does disaster bring out the failed humorist in you, Bel? But at least you don't have to waste your time sitting on a fake search committee. I guess we'll have to go to the Faculty Senate with this one, but I hear Danzig is trying to deconstruct the senate as well." Wendy's sigh was a long whine of resignation.

"He's probably afraid we'll mutiny. And if this sort of thing keeps up, we may very well have to. Try explaining to the accreditors why you've hired a Dumpster jockey to direct the Career Development Center. Oh well, at least you've taken my mind off poor Oscar Beckman."

Until Dr. G came, patronage had been pretty routine at RECC. We knew only too well that it was a virus that could spread throughout the college and infect everything from the quality of instruction to the availability of financial aid and adequate classroom space. The RECC faculty had been fighting this virus for decades. So both Wendy and I had a been-there-done-that response to patronage. Murder, on the other hand, was a different story altogether, one we had no firsthand experience with at all.

When I got home and clicked on the answering machine, I half expected to hear something sinister, an anonymous warning, perhaps a threat. But there was only a message from Marilyn, an old friend who worked in the bursar's office, setting up a lunch date for Tuesday. She sounded rather teary, so I left her a message agreeing to meet her at the RIP after my morning classes. Poor Marilyn. I figured she had suffered yet another setback in her perennially lousy love life. This was not sinister, just sad. But that night as I pored over the files, taking pages of notes to supplement my unreliable memory, it was not Marilyn I had on my mind but murder and murderers.

Chapter 11

November 1, 1994
Dear Professor Barrett:

The RECC Student Government plans to organize a permanent memorial in honor of Dr. Garcia. We are not sure if it should be a plaque or a scholarship or what. But we have formed a committee to work on it, and we are conducting an informal survey. We would like you to be an ex-officio member of our committee. We are going to poll the students, and we would like you to get some idea of what the faculty and administration want. Please let me know if you are willing to help us.

Yours truly,
Jennifer Seton, Chairperson
Dr. Altagracia Garcia Memorial Committee
Student Government Office, ext. 1193

After Illuminada observed my class on Tuesday, I had hoped we could share impressions, but as it turned out, she had to drive to Atlantic City in pursuit of a lead in a child support case she was working on.

So as soon as we had dragged the cartons of files out-side and heaved them into the trunk of her car, Illu-minada took off. This was probably just as well because I felt compelled to respond to Marilyn's SOS. I headed for the RIP.

Years ago, even before I met Sol and Marilyn found her latest Mr. Wonderful, we had formed our own version of a mini singles support group. Over count-less lunches at the RIP we had shared strategies and stories as we both struggled to come to terms with life after divorce for the woman over forty. Until she met her current partner about a year ago, my bright, attractive, warm, and sensitive friend had dated a string of louts and losers.

Marilyn was waiting. I was disturbed to note her puffy eyes and red swollen nose. She's usually svelte and soignée, but that day she looked like the before picture in a makeover promo. Her brown hair was dull and unkempt, her dress drab and baggy. I was especially upset to see her smoking, a habit she for-swore years ago. Sliding into the booth and squeezing Marilyn's hand, the one clenched into a fist around a Kleenex, I said, "So start at the beginning." I ordered chicken soup, tuna melts, and cups of hot water for us both.

"Shit, Bel, I thought Paul was going to marry me. We'd been living together for six months. He said he left his wife for me and we never so much as had an argument. We like the same jazz, the same movies. He was so sweet and protective. I never told you much about him because he's a pretty big deal, and his divorce wasn't final. He's Paul Ratstein, you know, on the RECC board, the 'friend of develop-ment' who's also the building inspector in Hoboken? You know who I mean?"

I nodded, hoping my face masked my incredulity as I pictured the stooped and skinny fifty-something-year-old with the wispy graying hair gathered into a straggly tail at the nape of his neck, his pointy profile exaggerated by his protruding incisors. "Try your soup."

"Bel, we even traveled together. He was so sweet to Ginny when she was home on vacation. I thought he really cared about me. When my old Mazda gave out, he even got me a college car." At this declaration, Marilyn flushed and played with her spoon before rushing on. "Oh, I know it wasn't right. The Subaru, I mean. But the college used to lease lots of cars, and he saw to it that I got one. And I figured it wasn't really hurting anybody, so I used it. I didn't get to keep it long anyway. After Garcia took over she reviewed the RECC car lease agreements. Of course, she couldn't see why an accountant in the bursar's office needed a college car. I never saw Paul so mad. He couldn't believe she canceled the lease on that car and had it returned without so much as a telephone call to him. He was fit to be tied."

"Taste your soup before it gets cold."

"I told him I didn't care. I'd saved enough to put a down payment on a Toyota by then, so I did. But he was still pretty upset. He tried to argue with her, but she kept talking about ethics and the budget. He took it very personally. I'm just glad she didn't hold it against me. I explained I had nothing to do with it and that I hadn't known it was a problem. What a fool she must have thought I was."

With great difficulty, I repressed a primordial urge to fill a spoon with broth and bring it to Marilyn's lips.

"Anyway, I went out to dinner last week with my

sister and her husband. Paul didn't want to go. He hardly ever wanted to go places with other people. He preferred not to share me, he said." At this, Marilyn's lower lip began to quiver, and tears splashed into her untouched chicken soup and onto the paper placemat.

I reached over and brushed them away with a napkin. "Why not try a little tuna melt? I won't let you finish talking if you don't eat something."

Obediently, Marilyn cut off a bite of her sandwich. But after only a mouthful, she put down her knife and fork and lit another cigarette. Finished with my own meal, I got out my fan and systematically directed the smoke away from us. I knew how her tale would end, but I wanted to hear it anyway. I also knew that the story's sleazy protagonist stood to lose a little more of his power over the teller each time Marilyn described his pathetic midlife shenanigans. "So what happened?"

"He said he had work to do, that he had to stay at the office. You want to know what really happened? I called him there just to say hi and tell him how much I missed him. I called from the phone near the bar at Laico's, and right while his machine was talking, I saw him in the mirror. He was with a beautiful girl." Again, Marilyn's mouth contorted and her eyes filled. "She was really young. Not much older than my Ginny. Not even thirty. They were sitting side by side, very close, in a booth. He was all over her. They couldn't see me. I was watching them while the tape on his machine ran. I couldn't believe what I was seeing. Then I went back into the ladies' room and threw up."

By the time the hot water for our tea came, Marilyn was leaning back in her seat looking spent. I dropped a Soothing Moments tea bag into her cup. I had my usual Orange Spice. "Anyway, he'd been cheating on me just like he cheated on his wife and God knows who else. And on top of that, I just found out that he didn't really leave his wife for me. She caught him with a friend of their daughter's and threw him out. *She's* divorcing *him*." I made a mental note to suggest that Marilyn get tested for HIV, but decided to wait until she was stronger before introducing that specter. "I suppose I'll have to get tested for HIV now," Marilyn blurted, taking me by surprise. "I feel so tacky. He was a scumbag from day one, and I just didn't get it.

"And now, as if that's not enough, I have to worry because he's still on the RECC board, and I don't want to end up out of a job. You're so lucky you have tenure. I just hope the Miss Teenage America he was with has a job. If not, he might be planning to give her mine. Do you know who that SOB's brother-in-law is? Remember Sammy Dworkin?"

"The ex-congressman? The geezer with the beer belly?"

"Yeah. He's married to Paul Ratface's older sister Maxine. And he's got some kind of chronic health problem, a heart condition or something. So he needs a job with a pension, a car, you know the drill. Guess what job he wants?"

"I give up. Not yours I hope?"

"Are you kidding? He wants to be president of RECC. Can you believe it?"

"But he has absolutely none of the qualifications of a college president," I practically shrieked, at last losing my carefully maintained facade of calm. "I mean none, nada, zilch." Even as I ranted, I recalled the résumé Wendy had described.

"That's what I said. But according to Paul he does have one major qualification. A lot of people owe him favors. I know he got Paul the building inspector job by campaigning for DeVito when DeVito ran for mayor of Hoboken the first time way back when. Paul made a joke of it, saying Maxine wouldn't let Dworkin in her pants until he took care of Paul." Marilyn was speaking faster now, anger alternating with self-pity, a good sign if you ask me.

I certainly hadn't expected to learn anything pertaining to the murder of Altagracia Garcia during lunch with Marilyn, but I'd been wrong. Maybe trustee Paul Ratstein, a dirty old man with a grudge and an out-of-work in-law, was literally a lady killer. After all, he, along with the other board members, had been at the fateful festival. "Drink your tea," I said.

When I got back to the office, Wendy was at her desk sputtering into the phone, "Well, Harold, you're wrong. This *is* an issue for the Faculty Senate. Last night at the special board meeting Danzig and the trustees made a mockery of the search committee, of the whole search process, in fact. There were only two faculty members on the committee to begin with. So even though we both voted against this cretin, it didn't matter. The rest of the committee supported him, and Danzig actually said, 'RECC students need a navigator with vision and experience to help them plot their courses on the storm-tossed seas of the work world in the nineties.' Don't laugh, Harold. It's not funny. He presented this trash collector as a candidate 'with several years' experience in both the public and private sectors.' Seriously, Harold. Now that Dr. G is gone, we're going to have to speak up or we'll be right back where we started." Wendy paused, listening to Harold, her shrugging shoulders and rolling eyes registering her impatience and frustration.

"Harold, listen to me. You know the grant we got? For the facilities needs assessment and a site search? They appointed committees to organize both of those. There are no faculty members on either of those committees, Harold, not a single one. And they'll be giving out contracts to consultants soon. Just remember, Harold, you heard it here first. We should at least have a special senate meeting to talk about all this. Think about it." Wendy slammed down the phone.

Chapter 12

To: Menopausesupportgroup@powersurge.com
Subject: Incontinence
Date: Fri, 4 Nov 1994 16:32:08
From: Bbarrett@circle.com

Anybody have any good ideas on how to keep my, shall we
say, relaxed and laid back uterus from bumping into my bladder every time I sneeze, cough, or laugh? I realize a dropped
uterus is not caused by menopause, but I don't have time to join
another mailing list every time a different body part rebels. Tuesday in class I sneezed from chalk dust, an occupational hazard,
and wet my pants! I have read about doing those vaginal muscle contractions when I'm driving or watching TV or on the
phone, but I've never been able to pat my head and rub my
stomach at the same time, let alone contract my vaginal muscles
while I'm trying to weave through rush hour traffic or make an
appointment with a student. Besides, my memory is so bad I
never remember until I'm mopping up. Is there anything else
anybody has tried? Let me know! I'm desperate!

The rest of the week was a blur. I sweated through
one particularly maddening session of the Academic

Council where there was an endless debate over whether the college's two decrepit vans were insured to transport students on local field trips. As I fanned and counted kegels, aging lechers, crashing cars, and Dr. G's contorted corpse whirled through my brain. Even though by Friday my car was fixed, Betty insisted on picking me up and driving me to Illuminada's. As usual there was no arguing with her. I was too tired to resist anyway.

The Gutierrezes live in a row house in Union City, about ten minutes away. Entering their living room, I felt as if I had left the twentieth century behind and was in a medieval palace. There were elaborately carved thronelike chairs, a plump sofa of burgundy brushed velvet with a complement of embroidered pillows, and on the walls, tapestries and an arrangement of portraits in ornate gilded frames. As I oohed and aahed, Illuminada beamed. Even Betty was running her hand over the carving on the chair nearest her.

"Raoul is a junkie. He loves junk. He finds all this stuff at flea markets or even on the street and fixes it up. He knows how to do upholstery and everything. Isn't he amazing? Accountant by trade, junk collector at heart. *Caramba!* I keep threatening him with one hell of a garage sale, but he won't part with anything." Even though Illuminada's words were complaining, she sounded proud of her husband. "He's with a client tonight, but he'll be back later for dessert with us and my mother. She lives upstairs."

As she talked, Illuminada motioned us into the kitchen. Here I was suddenly back in the 1950s. There was a Formica-covered chrome table with matching chairs. With a pang, I recognized a gleaming Waring blender, a Mixmaster, and a meat grinder identical to those that had been fixtures in my mother's Passaic kitchen forty years ago. Illuminada poured our sherry, and we carried our glasses and the bottle into the living room. We settled around the coffee table, an etched copper tray resting on what looked like a varnished tree trunk. The cartons of files waited on the floor.

Before we were even seated, I started pouring out the story of the Rollerblader, my nightmare, and my subsequent realization that someone really was trying to harm me. Up until then I'd resisted the temptation to dwell on this interpretation of events. This was not the first time that Bel Barrett, denial queen, had rejected a reality that was psychically unacceptable. I flashed my fan, sipped my sherry, and found comfort in Illuminada's frown and Betty's pursed lips. Like Marilyn, I felt relieved for having told my tale.

When Betty opened her mouth to respond, I cut her off, "Just one more thing. Tuesday I had lunch with . . ." As I recapped Marilyn's sad story, Illuminada listened attentively while, at the mention of Ratstein's name, Betty opened her laptop and began to type. When I finally wound down, we sat quietly for a moment before Betty broke the silence.

"Yes, Lord! Ratstein is a definite possibility. He hated Altagracia. Even before the car thing. You know how stunning she was? Well, he tried to move on that girl as soon as she got here. She was pretty insulted. There she was, trying to conduct a meeting, and he's groping and patting and leering. After that I always sat him at the opposite end of the table at board meetings. I'd forgotten about him. And that's not the sort of thing that would be in here." Betty pointed with her foot to the carton of files.

Illuminada interjected, "I'll see what I can get on

him. I know several clerks at city hall in Hoboken. It would be interesting to know his whereabouts when Bel's car was messed up." Illuminada poured another round of sherry and asked, "What's the best way to pool our responses to these files?"

On cue, Betty whipped out a sheaf of papers. With a flourish, she distributed spreadsheets. On the left side were names and on the right were blank boxes for recording data. The woman is anal beyond belief. I closed my gaping mouth and hoped my irritation didn't show.

"This should help. Then I can enter everything on my computer, and keep it all straight." As she spoke, Betty actually fondled her little electronic pal and, I swear, flexed her fingers. "I'll read a name. Then let's just brainstorm and see which people we need to check out further." In her take-charge mode, Betty did not pause for even a second to see how her approach sat with me and Illuminada. "Cesar Nuevos!" She pronounced this name with the ceremony of a sergeant-at-arms.

"Former dean for Enrollment Services," I called out. Why did I feel like I was on the *Gong Show* or playing charades? "Dr. G demoted him back to the classroom."

Betty elaborated crisply. "Yes, I remember. She couldn't fire him because he had tenure, so she demoted him. She made him a member of the ESL faculty. Nuevos literally refused to come to work, let alone teach. He used up all his sick days and resigned. Was Altagracia ever relieved to see him go! She took me out to lunch to celebrate. Then we organized a national search for an experienced enrollment manager." I guess it was the memory of this coup that made Betty flash a triumphant smirk my way.

"Dom Tarantello." I yelled out the name first in what I admit was a chidish urge to outmaneuver Betty. It was my turn to be "it," damn it.

"Well, chiquitas," Illuminada chimed in, apparently oblivious to my efforts to one-up Betty. "I heard a rumor that his nephew's getting a position at RECC. My sources tell me he'll be making more money than any of us." Betty typed feverishly.

I groaned. "You're right. He applied for a job, even though he's totally unqualified. My friend Wendy was on that search committee. He was railroaded through." My voice lowered a little.

"Sounds like a whole new ballgame to me," said Betty, calm in the face of my challenge.

"You better believe it, *chiquita*," said Illuminada, nodding her head in Betty's direction. Then Betty called out the next name, embellishing it with a little wave of her hand, "Commissioner Tom Koladnar, homey success story."

"He's not even in the files," said Illuminada.

Betty persisted. "I know that dude made a few phone calls to Altagracia regarding jobs for some of his constituents."

"Really?" Now she had my attention. "What did Dr. G say?" I could tell Betty enjoyed having privileged information. What a diehard control freak she was!

"She always told him his people were free to apply and be considered by the search committees. He wasn't real happy with her response. He kept telling her to skip the national searches and 'hire local,' but when she didn't, he never lost his cool. In fact, they worked together to get the grant money from the state. He was real helpful then." She paused dramatically, even her busy fingers suspended in midair. "I think he's a question mark." She said this definitively, clearly having the last word.

"Nelson Danzig." It was Illuminada, moving us right along. If she was aware of my reaction to Betty, she showed no sign.

At the mention of the name of her new boss, Betty blurted out, "This joker is virtually unemployable anyplace else in the world. Except maybe on the *Titanic*. But he just got a $15,000 raise. And"—she spit out her words faster and faster—"he has almost unlimited license to make the world's worst speeches whenever he wants. As far as bosses go, I've gone from the sublime to the ridiculous. Altagracia was going to do a national search to replace him too. He hated her." As if exhausted by her own outburst, Betty was suddenly silent.

"Guess you don't like him," said Illuminada archly, and the three of us giggled and guffawed until I had to make a run for the john. As soon as I I got back, Illuminada resumed our roll call, "Dwayne Smith Jr."

I noticed that my sherry glass had been refilled. I didn't mind so much that Betty was talking again. Her voice had less of an edge to it now. "Registrar. He claimed Altagracia dissed him because she didn't like the way he managed registration. She held him accountable loud and clear. Would you believe, he actually claims she was biased against African-American men? She broke up when she read the grievance he filed through his union. She was waiting for just the right moment to tell him that her dad was African. He hated her." On her last words, Illuminada and I chimed in, making the now familiar refrain a chorus.

It was my turn, so I called out, "George Morgan." Betty picked up on his name, saying, "Most of the faculty appreciated Altagracia, but that dude, he had to be an exception."

"Yes. He sure was." I smiled at the memory of George. "He was an early casualty of her ruling that a full-time faculty member at RECC cannot hold a full-time teaching gig anywhere else. Imagine that!"

Illuminada looked curious, so I continued, "When he refused to give up his other full-time position at NJIT where he was also an associate professor, Dr. G fired him. Want to guess how he felt about her?" By now I was waving the empty bottle, and Illuminada and I were slouched on the sofa, giddy with sherry and fatigue.

"Last but not least." It was Betty again. "Let's not forget Ratstein!"

"Break time, *senoras*! I want to go to sleep dreaming of beautiful women, so let's have dessert with Mamacita and then I'll crash and you can stay up all night if you want. Mina, your *mami*'s been waiting all evening to meet your friends." Raoul's good-humored entrance was hard to ignore, and his call to dessert irresistible. "*Mamacita*" turned out to be Milagros Santos, Illuminada's mother, who had come downstairs from her own apartment into the Gutierrez kitchen, where she was serving homemade flan and coffee. Raoul gave the tiny gray-haired woman a bear hug and a kiss.

The ensuing half hour was a welcome relief as we wolfed down the smooth sweet flan and savored the strong coffee. It was a given that tonight none of us wanted decaf. In fact, I couldn't wait for the moment when the combined hits of caffeine and sugar would kick in, energizing me for the late-night strategizing to come. Meanwhile, in the time warp of the warm kitchen, we relaxed. I was picking Raoul's brain about which flea markets to visit in search of antique china shoes for my collection when Betty stood up. "Party's over, gang. Let's get back to work."

By the time Betty dropped me off at well after two, my caffeine and sugar high had dissipated. Exhausted, I collapsed into a deep and dreamless sleep.

Chapter 13

To: Menopausesupportgroup@powersurge.com
Subject: Dry, Drier, Driest
Date: Sat, 5 Nov 1994 08:45:25
From: Bbarrett@circle.com

So what works on the dry eyes? I wake up in the morning feeling as if my eyelids are in need of a lube job. At the pharmacy there are at least twenty different kinds of eyedrops. Which one should I use? I hate eyedrops. Is there anything else that will help?

Of course, my eyes aren't my only body parts in need of irrigation. Sol and I have tried the vaginal lubricant Selena suggested, Easy-in, and then we tried Gyneglide that Helen likes. Later we're going to try Sexlax, the kind Charlotte swears by. Sol is enormously relieved that I don't cry during sex anymore. Seriously, they all seem to work, but we're committed to continuing our rigorous research.

No, I haven't had a chance to check out a new gynecologist or to do any more reading on HRT. We just finished midterms, and what with everything else going on here, I've been swamped. I'm glad Jeanette has had such good results with the patch. Keep in touch.

That same weekend I had another big scare. I was sound asleep for a change when suddenly I heard the scratchy squeak the front doorknob makes because nobody's oiled it since we moved in. Seconds later, I heard the sound again. This time I was fully awake. Years of lying in bed anxiously listening for Mark to come home from parties, clubs, and jam sessions have fine-tuned my nervous system. But Mark had flown the nest long ago. So who was trying to get in? The demon Rollerblader who ran me down in Liberty State Park? The psychotic who wrecked the brakes on my car?

I was literally scared stiff, so I had to force myself to slowly swivel my head and open my sandpaper-lidded eyes just wide enough so I could squint at my bedside alarm. It was the middle of the night, 3:10 to be exact. Scratch. Squeak. I heard it again. I knew I wasn't imagining that sound. Someone was actually turning my front doorknob. I felt sweat gather under my breasts and heat radiate throughout my trembling limbs. The sound stopped. Then I felt myself tense up again. From the window in the front room just below, I heard a scraping noise. It was very soft, but I knew exactly what it was. Someone was trying to pry open the front window.

Scooping up Virginia Woolf with one hand, I picked up the phone with the other and, huddling under the covers, dialed 911. Practically breathless with terror, I gasped into the phone, "Someone's trying to break into my apartment at 205 Park Street in Hoboken. I'm alone here. Please send a squad car right away! My name is Sibyl Barrett. Hurry! Please!" I hung up before the switchboard operator could put me off with any time-consuming questions. Then sitting up in bed, with Virginia Woolf kneading my damp nightgown, I listened to that insistent scraping sound. Suddenly I heard a deep voice, and then another. The noise stopped, and then the doorbell chimed.

I dropped the cat, pulled on my robe, and lit the bedside lamp before I ran downstairs to the front door and peered through the peephole. "Open up. Police here." The circle of the peephole framed the capped heads of two police officers. I was almost crying with relief when I opened the door. Between the policemen with their guns drawn stood a short, disheveled, unshaven man. He wore no coat, so he was shivering. It was Sol. I was very glad to see him even though, standing between the two six-footers in uniform and shifting his weight from one foot to the other, he looked like an embarrassed adolescent in need of a bathroom. "Good morning, beautiful. Surprise." I threw myself into his arms, much to the consternation of the two cops, who shrugged their shoulders and holstered their guns.

Sol mumbled into my neck, "Fred flew into Baku a couple of days ago, and he can manage things without me for a few weeks. I can't manage without you at all, so I'm home for a while. I thought I'd surprise you for dinner, but my plane was delayed." Sol turned to the officers and continued his explanation, "My overcoat was stolen in the airport in Baku. I hung it over the door of a stall in the men's room, and when I turned around, it was gone. Sort of behind my back, if you get my drift. My keys were in my coat pocket. At least they didn't get my cash and my passport." So saying, Sol pulled up his sweater, exposing the body belt I had given him before he left. Now looking at me, he continued apologetically, "I thought maybe I could get in without waking you,

you know, through the window the way Mark used to when he forgot his keys."

I said, "God, you scared me to death! The only reason Mark got in all those times was that I left the window unlatched because I knew he always forgot his keys. I didn't want Mark to know I was waiting up for him, and he didn't want to wake me by ringing the bell." It was clearly not the time or the place to mention that I seemed to be on somebody's hit list, a fact which had made Sol's nocturnal prowling even more threatening than it might have been otherwise. Instead I just nattered on, "And if you had gotten in and come upstairs, I would probably have died of coronary arrest before I figured out that you weren't a burglar."

"Then I've been away too long." Thanking the policemen, we retreated into the warm house.

Over a late brunch on Sunday, I shared with Sol my latest fears about Mark's travel plans, detailing how I envisioned him dead or at least maimed on three continents. How I wallowed in Sol's nonjudgmental understanding and reassurance! He's such a good listener. Seduced by the spirit of openness that has always marked our relationship, I told him first about Altagracia Garcia's death. Then I told him how Betty, Illuminada, and I were trying to figure out who really poisoned her. I even explained about the Rollerblader and the brakes, keeping my tone light and spicing my story with humorous asides.

But as I had feared, Sol was not amused. He was appalled. Suddenly he was closeminded and hostile. He was yelling, "Who do you think you are, RECC's version of Kate Fansler at fifty-two? Some menopausal Miss Marple? This is not a story, Bel. This is real."

Sol never yells. My father yelled. Lenny yelled. I no longer do men who yell. He saw my face, and, in a much lower voice, he said, "Jesus, Bel, I didn't mean to upset you. It's just that I don't get it. You're afraid to let your twenty-two-year-old six-foot-three son out of your sight, but you expose yourself to all kinds of risks."

As Lenny used to say, "The best defense is a good offense." Ignoring Sol's dig about overprotecting Mark, I went on the offensive. "You go running around politically unstable Eastern Europe where God knows what might happen. It's all right for you to act like an overage refugee from a John Le Carré novel, but it's not all right for me to try to figure out what's going on in my own workplace? You get to be a balding John Smiley, but I'm a menopausal crazy, is that it?"

I had stood up, and now *I* was yelling. Even when I saw his hand move reflexively to his balding head, I couldn't stop. "When Wendy and I unionized the RECC faculty years ago, they slashed all my tires three times in six months! That didn't stop us. When I was president of the RECC Faculty Senate, the board tried to save money by closing the library two days a week. Guess who notified the press? Guess who got the students to strike and shut down the college for three days? That's the year I had to get an unlisted phone number."

"Bel, that was different. The stakes were lower. This is murder. You're way out of your league here. But I'm not going to argue with you anymore. At least not now." Sol looked tired, jet-lagged. The euphoria of his homecoming hadn't lasted very long. But just as I was beginning to soften, he resumed his argument from another direction. "Just tell me one thing. Why not go to the cops?"

"There's no point in going now. They'll ignore us. I told you, the police are convinced they've solved this case. But I promise we'll go to them as soon as we've figured out what's going on. And I also promise that we'll be careful. Meanwhile I have to do this. It's not only for the sake of the Beckman kid, but I'm just so sick of RECC being run by these sleazy lowlifes. Dr. G was trying to change things. Now she's dead. Isn't that a coincidence? Give me a break. And poor Oscar Beckman is being blamed. Let's get real. How can I teach there without at least trying to figure out who really killed her?"

I resumed my seat across the kitchen table and poured us each another cup of tea. In a more measured voice, I continued. "You know, Illuminada's a very tough cookie. She's very sensible and has such good judgment. She has lots of experience with this sort of thing. And Betty's smart and really competent. It's not as if I'm operating in a vacuum. We're working together. When you meet them, you'll see." I could tell Sol was not reassured, but in the face of my resolve he knew there was nothing he could do. He didn't want to come off as another version of Lenny. And of course, we both knew he would continue to travel to Eastern Europe in spite of my concern for his safety in such a volatile part of the world.

"Bel, I'm going to worry now every time you're five minutes late getting home." He paused and took my hand. "Let me get you a cellular phone and promise to keep it with you. Program it to call 911. How about it? Will you at least do that? If not for yourself, for me?"

 *Chapter 14*

To: Bbarrett@circle.com
Subject: Mallomars
Date: Sun, 6 Nov 1994 20:44:16
From: Rbarrett@UWash.edu

Hey! It's been a while since I heard from you. Hope nothing's broken in Hoboken. Between your hot flashes and Dr. G's murder and midterms, I guess you're probably a little stressed. If you hadn't sent the awesome care package of Mallomars to get me through exams, I'd be really worried about you. But as long as you remembered that fall is Mallomar season, I know you're okay. Remember once when I was about ten, we bought a box of Mallomars on the same day they resurfaced at the supermarket in October? We took them up to Stevens and pigged out on them at the picnic table overlooking the skyline. You said something like, "This is the best of all possible worlds, Rebecca, Mallomars, and Manhattan." The entire rest of the year, you wouldn't even let Mark and me eat Fruit Loops and you rationed our M&M's intake, but you sure were were a wild woman when it came to those little chocolate-covered sugar cushions, weren't you? I hope you got yourself some too.

Anyway, thanks. Since you weren't here, I shared them (don't you think sharing is a little overrated?) with Stephanie while we were studying for our Physics I exam. Maybe that's why I got a 92! Now a new quarter has begun and I'm up to my seagreen eyeballs in more physics and psych. I sure hope I get accepted to physical therapy school when I finally apply after sweating through all the prereqs. Sometimes I wonder what a nice former classics major like me is doing in all these science courses. I guess now I'm a recovering classics major. I was so young when I was an undergraduate, wasn't I?

Oops, gotta go meet Keith. He's giving me a ride to the restaurant. Did I tell you he's thinking of training for a triathlon? Bye now. Be a good cybermom, and e-mail me soon.

Love,
Rebecca

I had managed to get an appointment for Wednesday morning with RECC's acting interim president Nelson Danzig by asking Betty to tell him I was calling as a member of the Altagracia Garcia Memorial Committee. Our meeting was predictably bizarre from the start. "Welcome to the bridge, Bel." He waved his arm around his office in an expansive gesture. "What's this about a memorial committee? Students' idea, no doubt." A frown creased his forehead.

I seated myself in the petitioner's chair across the desk from Danzig. Last time I had been in that office, it had been Dr. G's. Now it was stripped of her numerous diplomas and citations and the snapshots of her cowlicked son and dashing husband. The wall behind the desk was still covered with various photographs and certificates. But now the centerpiece was an enlarged and elaborately framed copy of Danzig's honorable discharge from the United States Navy. To the right of this was an even larger photo of a much younger Lieutenant Nelson Danzig in full dress uniform and to the left an equally grand picture of an enormous ship. Assorted flags decorated the wall across from the small window. On the desk were maps with colored lines charting what I assume were memorable voyages. Also on Danzig's desk was a bottle with a model of a ship imprisoned within. There was nothing immediately apparent to remind one that this was, in fact, the office of a college president, an educational leader. Rather, it looked like a naval officer's stateroom. I unfurled my fan, holding it ready to hide the smirk that I felt forming on my face.

"Thanks for making time for me. I know how busy you must be." I smiled what I hoped was an ingratiating smile. Then, covering half my face with my fan, I continued, "I want to pick your brain a bit about what you think would be an appropriate memorial for Dr. Garcia. As you know, students asked me to poll faculty and administrators, so, of course, I thought I'd talk with you first. They're thinking in terms of a scholarship in her name or a more tangible sort of memorial, maybe on the new waterfront campus she hoped we'd have someday. You had the chance to work with her so closely when you were acting dean for Business and Finance. I'm sure you must have lots of ideas."

Danzig leaned back in his chair, carefully positioned the fingertips of one hand on those of the other, looked right over my head at the wall behind me, and spoke slowly, solemnly, enunciating every single syllable, "Few understand what it really means to serve. Leadership is the most difficult form of service. She had no appreciation of the subtleties of command. Simply put, she didn't, couldn't run a tight ship . . ."

"Is it true that having a woman on a ship is bad

luck?" I interjected, widening my eyes in an effort to frame my loaded question in guilessness.

"Well look what happened once she came aboard!" Danzig sputtered, standing up and beginning to pace around the office, his hands still connected at the fingertips, his glance darting from the maps to the pictures, sometimes resting on the bottled ship. I tried to follow him with my eyes, peering intently over or around my fan. "She wanted to change everything. She had no respect for tradition. She humiliated people who had served this place for twenty years, since it was launched really! People like Cesar Nuevos and Dwayne Smith. You know Dwayne, Bel. Dwayne's been around forever. He knows how things work here. She insulted him. Right in front of some students and his staff. She didn't understand the chain of command, how to reprimand somebody without criticizing him."

He was pacing more rapidly now, and his voice was getting shrill and whiny. I encouraged him to go on. "It must have been difficult for you."

"Difficult?! Listen, Bel, even though you were an admirer of hers, I'm going to speak freely to you. I know whatever I say to you will go no further for the good of all concerned. After all"—Danzig looked at me and then gestured at the fleet of photos on the wall and added sotto voce—"loose lips sink ships." I nodded and fanned myself vigorously. He went on, "It was practically impossible to maintain order. She just kept wanting to change things. In less than a year, she changed our whole curriculum. She absolutely insisted on adding the liberal arts component. As if our students care about literature or learning foreign languages. Most of them already speak foreign languages. They just want to learn a trade. They don't need courses in philosophy or music or art. When I questioned her about it, she always turned my questions around. She had no respect for our traditions."

"What about her goal of getting a new campus for RECC on the waterfront?"

"More change. We've had some of these leases for nearly a quarter of a century. The board is very happy with the lease arrangement. The mayor likes it too. It wouldn't be good if he finds too many changes when he gets out. After all, our students don't need a campus. RECC is not the QE2, you know." He paused, looking fondly at the large photo of the ship behind me. "We're not the *Intrepid* either. We're more like this." Danzig pointed at the bottled boat on his desk, its voyages forever circumscribed by glass walls.

"I know the faculty liked her, Bel, and the students too. But you don't really understand leadership. Believe me, the view from the bridge is different."

"I'm sure it is," I nodded. "But I know you understand the students' desire for a memorial, especially considering the circumstances of her death. I mean, she didn't resign or even get fired. She was murdered." I watched Danzig's face closely as I spoke.

"Well, yes." Again wrinkles creased his forehead as he grappled with the "M" word. "It was very disturbing. Not good for enrollment. People don't want to sail on a vessel where there's been that kind of trouble. As for the memorial, I suggest a small plaque somewhere. Not a scholarship. Definitely not. We don't want to make a tradition of bringing up her name every year. That would just lead to bad publicity. A small plaque. Very appropriate." He resumed his seat, fingers of one hand again propping up those of the other, eyes on the wall. "Actually it's good of you to see to this, Bel. I know how many committees you serve on already."

"No trouble, really." I gathered that my audience was at an end, so I stood. Repressing an impulse to salute, I offered Danzig my hand instead.

Chapter 15

To: Menopausesupportgroup@powersurge.com
Subject: No More Sherry?
Date: Thurs, 10 Nov 1994 18:25:04
From: Bbarrett@circle.com

I just read Carmen's message about how when she gave up alcohol, her hot flashes diminished a bit. I considered following her example. Briefly. I mean, I like my sherry, let's face it, I really do. I'm not dependent on it, but I enjoy it. But let's look at the history here. I quit smoking in 1981. I gave up almost all coffee because of a thyroid problem I used to have. I'm trying to eat less red meat. I practically had to join a twelve-step program to wean myself off eggs for breakfast, but I finally did it. I no longer inject chocolate intravenously. And now you want me to give up alcohol? Just when the "experts" are saying a daily glass of wine is good for us? I don't think so. I'd rather sweat. But I'm glad it works for Carmen.

It hadn't been easy to arrange a meeting with Cesar Nuevos, former dean for Enrollment Services, another RECC rogue on our shortlist of suspects. He wanted little to do with RECC now. But I flattered him into agreeing to see me Thursday by hinting that I wanted him to address my Cultures and Values class on his pet topic, "The Immigrant and the Refugee: Different Dreamers of the Same Dream." He insisted that we get together at his apartment on Trini Lopez Boulevard in Union City, not far from Illuminada's.

As I drove along Kennedy Boulevard, I thought about Cesar. He was a dapper, nattily dressed man, near retirement age. A refugee from Cuba in the early sixties, he claimed to have once been a prominent attorney in Havana. Indeed, he was well connected in the upper echelons of Union City's extensive Cuban community. Within the confines of this close-knit group, he had never mastered enough written English to compose a comprehensible memo, proposal, or report. And his idea of college recruitment strategies had been to visit laundromats and bars, distributing registration forms to those he found there, apparently on the theory that a penchant for clean clothes and booze indicated an interest in and aptitude for higher education. Cesar had been openly contemptuous of these recruits, but he had never sought a more promising lot by visiting area high schools or businesses.

Cesar preferred to hire only staff members who were bilingual in Spanish and English, and then he'd encouraged them to speak mostly Spanish, totally mystifying the many non-Spanish-speaking would-be applicants who found their way to the RECC Admissions Office. His staff frequently complained that Cesar ran the office as if he were the dictator of a banana republic. For years they suffered as a result of their linguistic and professional isolation from the rest of the college. If Danzig was RECC's Lord Nelson, Cesar had been the college's Peron.

Cesar was notoriously macho. Betty had told me

how, on first meeting the regal Dr. Altagracia Garcia, he had addressed her in Spanish as "my little flower" and tried to kiss her hand. And long before the term *sexual harassment* became part of the lexicon on American campuses, Cesar Nuevos's female staff members had known better than to work late alone. I remember feeling grateful that now, at my age, at least I wouldn't have to worry about that from him.

But did the fact that he was an incompetent and a skirt chaser make him a murderer? Since his resignation, Cesar had not attended any RECC functions, including the ill-fated Fall Festival. So he would have needed a collaborator, someone who was at Liberty State Park that night, to do the actual poisoning. Was he capable of that? Had he hated Dr. G that much? I hoped my meeting with him would answer these questions.

With my new cell phone in my purse and with Betty and Illuminada both aware of my destination, I felt calm as I parked about a block away from the address Cesar had given me. Following his directions, I walked down the quiet street lined with neat pastel row houses. In this neighborhood, like Illuminada's, you had only to walk a block or two in any direction to get the best Cuban sandwich north of Miami. But even though I was tempted, I forced myself to attend to the job at hand. Noting the "For Sale" sign wired to the wrought-iron railing, I climbed the stoop stairs and pushed forcefully on the buzzer of 9814.

I was completely taken aback when a stunning middle-aged woman opened the door. She was classically elegant in a gray cashmere skirt and sweater. I lusted after the double rope of pearls and matching earrings she wore. They set off her swirls of silver hair swept into a French knot. She smiled warmly and greeted me with her hand outstretched. "Professor Barrett? Welcome. I'm Graciela Nuevos, Cesar's wife." Ushering me into a lushly carpeted living room, Graciela helped me off with my coat and settled me into a comfortable chair, calling into another room, "Cesar, our guest is here."

"Thank you, my dear." RECC's notorious lech smiled lovingly at his wife and then at me. While Cesar went to the kitchen for sherry, I chatted with Graciela and checked out the photographs of children and grandchildren. My eyes lingered on a heart-shaped frame containing a small, slightly faded picture of a young man and woman in evening clothes staring besottedly into each other's eyes.

"That's Cesar and me at our engagement party." A wistful note crept into Graciela's voice. "We were so young, and life seemed so simple then. That was Cesar's family's home in the background. Remember, Cesar, how we danced on our engagement night?" Graciela addressed this question to Cesar, who had emerged from the kitchen with a small tray and three glasses of sherry.

"We are still young. And soon we will be dancing together every week." Putting the tray down, Cesar again smiled at Graciela.

The connubial closeness of my host and hostess, combined with the comfortable, rather formal room, had caught me off balance. I had never heard anything of Cesar's wife or family. In fact, I'd expected him to live alone in a flashy den of fuchsia satin and chrome, my admittedly cliched fantasy of an aging Latin Lothario's bachelor pad.

"It is wonderful that you want Cesar to speak to your students," said Graciela, effortlessly directing the conversation to what she thought was the purpose of my visit. "He still has so much to offer. He's a real resource, *un tesoro*. As a guest speaker, he can share with them his wisdom and experience." A slight accent lent a musical lilt to her words. She opened a seashell-shaped box ornamenting the table and withdrew a black silk fan with a handle studded with marcasites and began to gently fan herself. Now I could see that Graciela's soft features were gleaming with perspiration. Smiling, I withdrew my own comparatively plain fan, and began to pass it back and forth in front of me. Graciela and I smiled at each other in sweaty complicity as Cesar began to speak.

"Yes, I will be happy to address them, to explain to them what it is like to leave your country, your family, your youth even," he intoned, glancing at the small photo. "But I will tell them also of the possibilities of this great country, how with hard work and, of course"—he bowed slightly in my direction—"with education, you can fulfill your dreams. But, Bel, I should tell you, we must set the date not too far off. We have told few people yet, but we are soon to leave this area."

"Oh?" I looked at him and then at Graciela with an unspoken question in my eyes.

"Wait. I'll show you." And Cesar left the room.

Graciela refilled our glasses and, smiling fondly at Cesar's retreating back, said, "I'm so proud of him, at his age to be starting again. When he resigned, I was proud too. Cesar was too advanced in his thinking for that college. And that new president, she couldn't appreciate his level of thinking at all. I'm sorry she died, but I think others can lead the college much better, don't you?" Cesar's return spared me the dilemma of having to answer Graciela's question.

"You see, Bel, I have a new position. It's in Miami

at El Dorado. It's a country club for the Cuban community. I'm going to be the director. I'll be responsible for everything, the grounds, the social activities, the membership qualifications, the treasury, everything will be run by Cesar." Smiling broadly, Cesar poked his chest with his thumb for emphasis. "Of course, I'll have people to help me." Here he winked at Graciela. "But I will make the decisions." Handing me the letter containing his job offer, Cesar stood back glowing with pride.

"He was selected over many others. The Board of Directors there recognized his administrative experience and his charm."

While Graciela extolled her husband's virtues, I quickly noted the letter's date, August 16, 1994. He had been offered this directorship almost two months before the murder. I handed the letter back to Cesar, saying simply, "Congratulations. The position sounds perfect for you." I raised my glass to each of them in a toast. "How did you find out about this opportunity? Had you been looking for a long time?"

"Graciela's cousin is on the Board of Directors at this club. When he heard that I might be available, he begged me to come down to talk with the others. I had several interviews over the summer. Graciela and I, we have been to many dances and festivities at the El Dorado over the years. Both of us have relatives who are members. Family is very important, especially as we get older, don't you think? Graciela has already in mind a condominium she likes near her sister, isn't that right, dearest?" Cesar smiled engagingly.

"Well, let's plan a date when you can speak to my students soon then," I said reaching into my bag for my datebook. "The class meets Tuesday and Thursday mornings from 10 to 11:15. How about next Thursday?"

Later as I walked to my car, I was convinced that there must be two Cesar Nuevoses, so different was his home persona from that of the man I remembered from RECC. Was it the sherry? I doubted it. I was mulling over this riddle of the two Cesars as I walked along the darkening street. Lost in thought, I was slow to notice the figure flitting in and out of the shadows of the parked cars just behind me. But gradually the padded footsteps intruded on my consciousnesss. As they grew more audible, I chastised myself for worrying. I couldn't go through the rest of my life thinking that every footstep was an assailant.

Nevertheless, I reached into my bag, searching for the reassuring touch of my new cell phone. The footsteps were right behind me now. Just as I felt a pressure on my shoulder, I heard a car screech to a halt, the slam of a car door, and a vaguely familiar voice ordering, "Hold it right there or I'll shoot."

I froze. The hand on my shoulder froze. I didn't dare to move, especially when I saw in the light of the street lamp a trench-coated figure moving rapidly toward me, both arms straight out, hands holding a gun pointed right at me.

"Bel, move away so I can see who your new friend is." Now I recognized the voice as Illuminada's, and, as I moved aside, I could see her more clearly. "*Come mierda*, Betty! What the hell are you doing?" Illuminada screeched. I turned around, and there was Betty, a stocky figure in black sweats and sneaks. Those footsteps had been hers.

"What does it look like I'm doing? I'm keeping tabs on Bel so nothing else happens to her." Emerging from behind me, Betty went on. "I'm a black belt in tae kwon do, remember? And what the hell are you doing with that gun? Is that real? What is your problem, girl?"

"I've been following Bel too. I didn't recognize you." For a moment, I was stunned. When I had told Sol that Illuminada and Betty were tough and competent, I'd been trying to reassure him. It had never occurred to me that Illuminada owned a gun, let alone knew how to use it. I don't even approve of guns. And Betty had once mentioned offhandedly that she had taken tae kwon do right after her divorce. Of course she'd be a black belt. Damn, these two really were tough. And they had schlepped halfway across the county at the end of a busy workday to make sure nothing happened to me. I felt blessed.

Illuminada giggled as she casually dropped the pistol into her shoulder bag, and her giggle set us all off. Within seconds, there on the otherwise silent street, the three of us erupted into gales of nervous laughter. Soon tears were running down our faces and we were stamping our feet. Convulsions of relief and hilarity tore through each of us, and we continued our raucous stomping circle dance right there on the sidewalk. I was the first to cry out, "Stop! Stop or I'm going to wet my pants! I mean it! Stop!"

Chapter 16

To: Bbarrett@circle.com
Subject: Dad's Visit
Date: Tues, 15 Nov 1994 06:21:05
From: Rbarrett@UWash.edu

Dear Mom,

Guess who flew into Seattle on business? You're right, Dad. He called me and told me to make dinner reservations for Sunday night. He wanted to take Keith and me out for a fancy meal, but I had a test on Monday, so I suggested we make it Monday night. Keith and I are usually off Monday nights. Anyway, we went to Pescatore's, near the locks just north of here. It's a great seafood place with really sweet views of the canal. Of course, it was pouring, so we just admired the rain hitting the windows.

Dad didn't say anything about our apartment, but he seemed interested in Keith's bike, which we store in the kitchen. It's not a really big apartment, you know. But things were totally cool when Keith was asking Dad questions about business and tax breaks and stuff. Then Dad wanted to talk about the Sonics. Unfortunately Keith doesn't follow the team and neither do I, so there was a little down time until I got Dad talking about Cissie and how she's redoing their house again. He didn't seem too happy about that.

Dad was also complaining about Mark. He really doesn't want Mark to go into teaching. He kept saying, "Talk him into computers, Kitten. That's where the money is. You can talk to him."

Just before he left, Dad asked what you were up to. I didn't tell him. He'd freak if I told him you were trying to solve a murder.

Gotta go to class.

Love,
Rebecca

Betty, Illuminada, and I were nervous wrecks. In the kaffeeklatch at the RIP after our near shootout on Trini Lopez Boulevard, we admitted it. Even Betty told us that when Illuminada had pulled a gun on her, she had actually started reciting the Lord's Prayer. Maybe Betty was human after all. So anyway, I took the initiative and booked Illuminada, Betty, and me into the Tenth Street Baths for an evening of steam, soaking, and massage. The century-old Turkish bath house in the East Village sure ain't no Canyon Ranch, but it never fails to work its funky magic on me. I knew that on ladies' night at the baths we three could literally let it all hang out and relax for a few restorative hours.

And so on Tuesday night I drove us into Manhattan for a megadose of stress reduction. For starters we each enjoyed a no-nonsense Swedish massage. I requested special attention to the back of my neck and my shoulders, which of late had been knotted with tension. These rubdowns were followed by a session in the steam room, where, seated on our towels, we whooped with laughter as we relived our armed encounter with one another.

From time to time we emerged from the steam room to dabble our feet and hands in the small icy pool, brightly tiled by a long dead mosaic artisan. Illuminada actually dove in for a few seconds before surfacing, frozen and ready for more steam. We wandered in and out of the sauna too, exclaiming as the hot doorknob singed a palm or the dry heat entered our shriveled nasal passages. We even braved the inner recesses of the Russian steam room, where we sat on benches around the edge. Just as the heat seemed unbearable, we'd wet our towels under one of the cold water taps and let the chilled liquid drip down our sweating faces, backs, and breasts. Betty, ever in control, fashioned her soaking towel into a regal-looking turban, which ensured her a steady drizzle of coolness. Always there was the alternative of the icy pool. Finally we lowered ourselves into the hot tub.

Betty broke our companiable silence. To my surprise, the first thing she blurted out across the bubbles was, "Randy is unhappy at college. He wants me to go and get him and bring him home." When I looked quizzical, she explained. "He misses his girlfriend. He hates his roommate. He also hates the food, the cold, and"—here Betty banged her fist on the water—"he says the classes are too hard. Should I go?" I couldn't believe it. Ramrod Ramsey was actually asking advice. But I felt for her. There's nothing like a phone call from an unhappy college freshman to pluck the parental heartstrings, especially if, like Randy, he's your only kid.

Before I could answer, Illuminada spoke up. "*Dios mio.* Luz wants to come home every other week. One week she hates her roommate, the next they're best friends. She got an 82 on a chemistry test last week, and she never got below 95 on anything in high school. Also she says the water is giving her zits. And according to her, everyone in her dorm is an alcoholic." Illuminada threw her hands up in a classic gesture of helplessness, showering us with droplets of water.

"What do you say when she tells you all this? Does she want to come home?" Betty sounded genuinely curious.

I couldn't resist interrupting before Illuminada could reply. "For whatever it's worth, at first Rebecca thought her freshman roommate was an anti-Semitic sadist. Last June she was maid of honor at Tish's wedding. And Mark"—here, I couldn't suppress a snort of laughter—"spent most of his freshman year waiting for pizza to be delivered to his dorm or for his roommate and some girl to get out of bed so Mark could get into the room to sleep. The happy college freshman is a myth."

"You don't think I should let him come home?" Betty looked from me to Illuminada.

Illuminada responded firmly, "No. But tell him you'll discuss it with him Parents' Weekend or some other weekend. Then go up there and take him out to eat and listen to him talk. Don't say much. Don't argue with him. Be simpatico. Then tell him you'll discuss it with him over Thanksgiving. That's what we told Luz. She didn't like it, but she went along with it."

"And if you can, bring his girlfriend along. He'll get so into showing her around that he may even sell himself on the place," I added, splashing a little water in Betty's direction.

Betty seemed relieved and splashed me back. I

toyed with the idea of sharing my fear about Mark's future: his grim job prospects here and, even more disturbing, his plans to visit the unstable Middle East or work in the notorious canneries of Alaska. But I held back until I could be sure that this warmer, gentler Betty was for real. Instead, I shifted the subject. "Working for Lord Nelson has to be extremely nerve-wracking. The whole time I was talking to him, he didn't make eye contact with me. It was so strange. Have you started looking for another job?"

"You're right on, Bel. He's some nutty dude, a real piece of work. Half the time I feel sorry for him and the other half I want to kill him. He needs a keeper, not an executive secretary. As soon as we get things sorted out about Altagracia, I'll start looking, don't worry." Betty sounded so relaxed now, so tolerant of my curiosity and my light nag. It's too bad she couldn't have a massage and a soak every day.

"Bel, did you learn anything from your talk with Danzig except that he's not into eye contact?" Now Illuminada sent a splash of water in my general direction along with her question, the first direct reference of the evening to our joint undertaking.

"Not really. I mean, we know he's a nutcase too. But he didn't bat an eyelash when I mentioned the word *poison*. I didn't get the sense that he was hiding anything. He acknowledged very freely, very openly, how much he had disliked having Dr. G around. The board and the mayor must be thrilled to have him in her place; he's definitely their man. He doesn't have the brains to even pretend otherwise. Either that or he's a shrewd actor."

"Before we count him out, remember that healthy raise he just got," remarked Illuminada. "He's still a possibility in my book."

"What about Cesar?" Betty chimed in.

"Are you ready for this? He's going to be director of a Cuban country club in Miami! Is that too perfect? And he has a lovely wife, very chic and refined. About my age. Who would have guessed that? I don't think he did it. I think he hated and resented her, but he has a whole other life outside RECC with family and community respect. He got the country club job long before the murder and he wasn't even at the festival. At one point while I was there, I wondered if Mrs. Cesar was the culprit. She's so devoted and all. But she seems very happy to be Miami-bound. She's no Lady Macbeth. God, this feels good."

"Lord yes, but it's time to vacate. We're hogging the hot tub. Besides, I sure could use some dinner now and a cold beer. I'm beginning to feel like a raisin." So saying, Betty was the first to step out of the steamy cauldron and head for the shower. And somehow I didn't even mind. Later in Danal, a little nearer to Fifth Avenue, Betty was also the first to raise her stein of Amstel Lite in a toast to me, saying, "Here's to Bel for getting us into hot water!" Illuminada joined in while all three of us groaned at Betty's awful double entendre. Even though dinner was a backdrop for discussion of strategy, assignment of tasks, and endless speculation, our mood remained mellow.

Chapter 17

To: Menopausesupportgroup@powersurge.com
Subject: Moi! Moi! Moi!
Date: Tues, Nov 15 1994 24:15:08
From: Bbarrett@circle.com

Tonight I had a Swedish massage, the first one in years. I actually spent a few hours in a spa soaking, steaming, and pampering myself. It was so lovely. I feel born again, relaxed and comfortable in my skin. I feel as if I can do anything. Why don't I do the spa thing more often? Surely by now I've earned the right to spend a little time and money on myself once in a while? I mean, I have, haven't I? (Yes, I am looking for validation. Hurry, before the guilt sets in.)

Germaine Greer says the goal of "facing up squarely to the climacteric is to acquire serenity and power." Well, she's right! From now on I'm going to follow my bliss. Power to all us laid-back crones!

By Monday morning, my mellow mood was only a memory. My weekly walk with Wendy had been rained out. Preparing my midterm advisory grades had eaten into precious weekend time, so I'd not yet read whole sets of papers I had hoped to return to students. And instead of catching up on my essay reading, I had that damn meeting I'd scheduled with Dwayne Smith. No wonder I felt unusually harried waiting outside the registrar's office for Dwayne to receive me.

Nonetheless when Keisha Charles, the work-study student assigned to the registrar, motioned me in, I entered smiling and offered my cheek to be kissed. After all, Dwayne and I go way back. I had almost forgotten how big he was. The registrar was at least six feet, six inches tall, and I tilted my head so as not to waste the smile I had managed. "Hi, Dwayne. Thanks for making time for me. I'll only be a minute."

"You take your time, Professor. You've got me all to yourself now. What can I do for you?" He pulled out a chair for me and seated himself in another one across a low table so we faced each other. Now that I could see his face without doing a backbend, I was pleasantly reminded that Dwayne was not unaware of how to work a smile himself. Against his dark skin, Dwayne's white teeth flashed in a welcoming grin that said, "This smile is just for you. Enjoy it." I was. "Coffee? Tea? Danish?" My resolve to stick to business, and the diet I begin anew every Monday, melted. I opted for tea and a cheese Danish from the well-stocked tray my host offered. "Now, Bel, how can I help you?" Folded into the chair opposite me, Dwayne personified an easy graciousness.

On the other hand, with my mouth full of Danish, I could at first manage no more than a grunt. "Now, Professor, take it easy. I'm not going anywhere. You want me to change a room for you? Or shift a few folks out of one of those big sections you've got? Whatever. I'm here to help."

"Thanks. This is delicious. No. It's nothing like that, Dwayne, but I do finally have my midterm advisory grades to turn in personally," I said, handing him the large manila envelope containing my rosters and attendance sheets. I hoped he wouldn't carry on because they were a day late. I was relieved when he just nodded and tossed them onto his desk.

I flashed another smile of my own before beginning my pitch. "The Student Government asked me to be the faculty rep on a committee they've formed to establish a memorial for Dr. Garcia. I'm supposed to poll faculty and administrators. That's why I'm here, Dwayne, to see what ideas you have."

Dwayne Smith extended his long legs until he had positioned his heels on the edge of his desk in front of us. He sipped his coffee. His posture was so relaxed that the sharp, angry tenor of his next words caught me off guard. "Why're you asking me? I have no respect for her dead or alive. Talk to the rest of your pals on the faculty. She had a regular fan club there. You professors"—he spat out the word, confirming my sense that in his lexicon it was often an epithet of scorn—"you thought she was God, didn't you?" Before I could reply, he continued, "But she had a mean tongue in her head and no respect for those of us who've been here trying to keep this place going, doing the best we could . . ." Dwayne paused.

"You know, Bel, we're practically the only only community college in the state that doesn't have phone-in registration yet. Of course we have lines here at registration. And when our stone age computer goes down, we have lines to get in line. You've met Keisha out there? My work-study student? That young woman is my staff except for a part-timer in the evening. I go to conferences and the other registrars laugh when I tell them how we operate here."

As Dwayne warmed to his description, his voice got louder and he removed his feet from the desk and straightened up in his chair. Looking at me, he asked, "You've heard what she did to me, right? There are no secrets in this place."

I shook my head, justifying my fib by virtue of the fact that I had never actually heard the whole story, only that there had been a reprimand. "She came by here the first night of fall registration, right? Not only was the computer down, but the air conditioner too. Keisha, my part-timer Yousef, and I were sweating our buns off trying to process students. And none of us speaks Spanish either. How many times have I put in for a worker here who speaks Spanish? Yousef's good, but we've got to have someone fluent in Spanish, right?" I nodded and sipped my tea.

Encouraged, Dwayne continued. "So who comes charging in, jabbering away a mile a minute in Spanish to all the people in line? They were all excited and jabbering back at her. I could tell she was asking how long they'd been waiting. Then she screamed out, 'Who's in charge here?' and when I answered, she yelled, 'Serving these students has to be our first priority.' Like what did she think we were trying to do? And, damn it, Bel, if she didn't come behind the counter and start registering people herself as fast as she could."

There was little trace of Dwayne's mellow charm now. He sat tense in his chair and continued his tirade. "Soon she got her secretary, that Ramsey woman, working here with her, and those two registered students so fast. And the whole time they both shouted orders at Yousef and me. It just wasn't right to treat me, a credentialed professional, like that in front of Yousef and all those students. After all, Yousef reports to me."

Dwayne shook his head before continuing, "It's like the kids say. She dissed me. And Bel, you know and I know she would have treated me with more respect if I were white or even Hispanic. Then she'd have treated me like a professional." Dwayne sat back, as if deflated by his outpouring.

The image of the diminutive Dr. G and Betty commandeering registration from this towering official had me fighting a grin and fishing for my fan so I could hide my face. "I can see where you would have been upset," I ventured diplomatically. Then before he could reply, I went on, "I guess someone else felt the same way you did."

"Meaning what?" Dwayne seemed tense again, still bruised by even the memory of what he clearly perceived as a great humiliation.

Slowly I poured myself some more hot water and gestured toward Dwayne, "More coffee?"

"Thanks." He held out his mug while I refilled it from the carafe.

"Meaning someone hated her enough to poison her." I focused on his face and the hand holding the mug of coffee. His eyes met mine, and his hand remained steady.

"Yeah. They got the kid who did it. White kid, too. One of those punks from CAI. A discipline case. I wonder what he'll get." Dwayne turned toward a whiteboard behind him filled with figures. "Something like that could really hurt our numbers. So far though, early registration stats are the same as last year's. I'm keeping my fingers crossed."

"Me too. But what shall I report back to the committee? I mean, do you favor a plaque or a scholarship? Those seem to be the choices..." I looked inquiringly at Dwayne, waiting for his reply.

"Man, Bel, you sure don't give up, do you?" His eyes were twinkling now, and he seemed once again easy and cool. "If I get my way, there will be a one-word inscription on that woman's plaque." When I furrowed my brow into another questioning look, Dwayne grinned his easy grin again and spit out," 'Bitch.' "

# Chapter 18

To: Bbarrett@circle.com
Subject: Talking Turkey
Date: Sat, 19 Nov 1994 03:09:18
From: Rbarrett@UWash.edu

Mom,

If you have time in the next few days, would you please e-mail me the directions for making Thanksgiving dinner. I have to work at the restaurant on Thanksgiving, but Keith has off, so he wants to try making a turkey. He wants to do the whole traditional thing, sausage stuffing, scalloped oysters, apple pie, and everything. He even asked his mother to send her corn pudding recipe. When I get home from work that night with a pocketful of humungous holiday tips, we'll have a romantic Thanksgiving dinner for two. Isn't that awesome? You can skip the lima bean casserole recipe though. Gotta go to work.

Love,
Rebecca

The last thing I felt like doing the day after my chat with Dwayne was taking my Intro to Lit class on a field trip. But a promise is a promise, and we'd planned this outing the very first week of the semester. We were going to the main branch of the New York Public Library, in my opinion a must-see attraction beside which the Empire State Building, the Cathedral of St. John the Divine, and even the gilded Trump Tower pale. Although I must admit the subterranean marble ladies' room in the Trump Tower is my favorite midtown pit stop, but never mind that.

At least it wasn't raining, just raw, cloudy, and November-gray. The trip's logistics were simple enough. RECC is only a few blocks from the PATH train, which would whisk us from Jersey City and beneath the Hudson River to Thirty-third Street and Sixth Avenue in about twenty minutes. From there the library is a ten-minute walk. In spite of how easy it is to get to New York from Jersey City, few of my students venture in very often, and when they do, they don't go to the library. I was determined to show them how user-friendly the Apple is and how sexy a really great library can be.

By departure time, twenty of my twenty-six students had arrived, several carrying cameras. I was disappointed to note that Rowanda and Frank were not among them. As soon as I had locked their book bags in my office, we began our ragtag procession to the PATH. Rowanda caught up with us on the subway platform, breathless but grinning.

I settled into a seat next to her on the nearly empty post-rush-hour train. "I enjoyed your midterm, Rowanda. The way you contrasted Lady Macbeth and Hillary Clinton was original and made me think, especially the part about how Lady M was not big on

nurturing and Hillary is. I'm looking forward to reading your *Macbeth* paper. How's it coming?"

Rowanda's grin faded a little and she said, "I need
to get started on it. I got a job in the after-school program at my mother's church now. It take up a lot of
time, but it help a lot with bills. I can bring my son
there. He like it with all the toys and the other kids.
I'll get to that paper this weekend maybe."

"How is your son?" Of course, I couldn't recall the
child's name. On cue, Rowanda whipped out a snap-
shot of an adorable toddler with just the right com-
bination of dimples, rolls of thigh fat, ringlets, and
eyelashes. My long-repressed inner grandmother was
in real danger of getting out as I ogled that baby. He
was in the arms of a beaming young man. "He's precious and getting bigger all the time. And who, may
I ask, is this happy-looking guy?" I figured Rowanda
wouldn't have shown me the photo if she didn't want
me to ask, right?

"That Jamal's father. He outta jail now. He stop by
sometime to see his baby. He was in this program for
young fathers in jail. So sometimes he come by. He
say if he get a job, he gonna help support Jamal. We
see." There was not even a trace of Rowanda's grin
now. In fact, she wore her serious expression, the one
which made her look so much older than I knew her
to be.

"Are you sure it's just Jamal he comes to see?" So
I'm intrusive and nosy. Again Rowanda didn't have
to answer, but she did, so softly that I could barely
make out her words over the roar of our train. "It
don't make no difference. My mother don't like him.
And she on dialysis now. Me and Jamal, we back
livin' with her, so we can keep an eye on her, see she
take her medicine and get to those treatments. She

don't like Jamal's father 'cause he got busted for joy-ridin'. She say he a criminal and that he a bad influence on Jamal."

The thought of nineteen-year-old Rowanda being responsible for her child and her sick mother while working and going to school full-time was a grim reminder of the hardships so many of my students face. Could Rebecca, who was five years older, cope with all that? And here I was nagging Rowanda about finishing a paper. Before I could get too conflicted, we were in New York and walking toward Fifth Avenue.

Concepcion and I strode along together. As usual she was chatty. "Did you see in the paper last night? RECC just hired that big consulting firm the mayor uses, Architecture Associates, I think is their name, to look for a site for our new campus. They're going to pay them $75,000 for six months' work. Wow! I would have to work six years to make that kind of money."

"No, Concepcion, I didn't get a chance to look at the paper yesterday. That's interesting though. That money must be coming from the grant Dr. Garcia wrote shortly before she died. I guess there was another special board meeting. I wonder what else was decided." Concepcion was delighted to satisfy my curiosity.

"Not that much. But they did form a search committee to find a new president. They picked all trustees and a commissioner and some aide from the mayor's office. You'd think they'd have at least one student on that committee, wouldn't you?" Concepcion sounded aggrieved.

"Well, yes, and maybe even a few faculty members too," I answered, sounding not a little aggrieved myself.

"That's the way Dr. Garcia would have done it,"

said Concepcion. "She was always trying to get us students to participate in things, right, Rafik?" Rafik had come up behind us, and Concepcion had linked arms with him.

"You talking about Dr. Garcia I guess? Yeah, she was always after us to join clubs and march in Trenton about our budget and just get involved." Rafik sounded wistful and shook his head as he spoke. "Lord Nelson, who's taking her place now, he don't seem too involved himself."

Soon we stood between Patience and Fortitude, the most famous of New York's literary lions, and Concepcion handed her camera to a surprised tourist and persuaded her to take our picture. As we climbed the stairs, everyone seemed appropriately impressed by the grandeur of the library's sculpted facade and the sheer scale of the place. I overheard Rafik mutter something about the pyramids. He had left Egypt at four and returned only once since then. Clearly the library was triggering his memories of the world's other wonders, and we hadn't even gone in yet.

Our docent had just gathered us around her in Astor Hall, the library's majestic but totally bookless lobby, when I heard a familiar voice. "Yo! Professor Barrett!" Frank O'Leary, backward baseball cap askew, face flushed, and both thumbs up, slid into a spot between Rowanda and Rafik. I'd left the library's address and travel directions on the board in the unlikely event that any latecomers elected to meet up with us, and here was Frank. Let the tour begin.

And what a tour it was! Rafik was fascinated by the notion of sneakered pages delivering books from the underground stacks to researchers on request. He kept muttering, "Eighty-eight miles of books! That's a lotta books." Rowanda lingered for a long time at the special exhibition of early illustrated manuscripts, running her finger back and forth over the glass cases that cradled them. The reading room astounded everybody. It wasn't so much the patina of the old wooden tables or the soft lighting or even our docent's stories of famous authors who had written their famous books at those very tables that got to them. Rather it was the spectacle of rows of people, young and old, sitting there of their own free will in the middle of the day reading. Concepcion marveled at the fact that anyone, even people from New Jersey, could use the library for research. She actually looked a little teary when we read the inscription recognizing the contribution of Martin Radtke, a Lithuanian immigrant. He credited the library with having enabled him to "educate himself." To express his gratitude, Radtke at his death left much of the fortune he earned to the library. To tell the truth, that inscription always makes me a little teary too.

After his exuberant entrance, Frank had been quiet, listening attentively, but not oohing and aahing with the rest of us. On the walk back to the PATH station, I inquired, "So, Frank, I'm glad you were able to get here. What did you make of the place?"

"It's totally awesome, man. It makes even the library at state look cheesy. And our RECC library." He snorted derisively before going on. "The entire RECC library would fit in the gift shop we just saw. I can't wait to hear what the accreditors are going to say this spring when they come. I heard Lord Nelson formed an SOS Committee. You want to know what SOS stands for?"

I was not at all sure that I did want to know, but Frank's query had been purely rhetorical because he continued without even a pause, "Save Our School.

They're supposed to be in charge of preparing for when the accreditors visit." Frank snorted again. "Excuse my language, Professor Barrett, but at RECC SOS means Same Old Shit just like it does anyplace else, only nastier."

Loritza approached me on the train ride back to Jersey City. Hanging on to an overhead strap with one hand, she fumbled in her pocket with the other and pulled out a crumpled sheet of paper. "Professor Barrett, a few of us are trying to raise money to help Ozzie Beckman's family pay his legal fees, people from my church who know him and some other RECC students too." At Grove Street a man seated next to me got up to leave, and Loritza took his seat and continued, "We're having a fund-raiser, a covered-dish party, at the church in a couple of weeks. Can I pass this announcement around in class next week and say something about it? It won't take long." When I nodded my assent, I refrained from mentioning how many covered-dish suppers it would take to make a dent in what Oscar's legal fees would add up to if . . . But I didn't let myself finish that thought. It stayed with me though, long after the train pulled into Jersey City and my train companions had all retrieved their book bags and gone their separate ways.

 *Chapter 19*

To: Menopausesupportgroup@powersurge.com
Subject: Vaginal Appliances (I'm Serious) and My Weight
Date: Tues, 22 Nov 1994 23:48:19
From: Bbarrett@circle.com

I'd rather do kegels than lift "tamponlike weights" with my pelvic floor muscles, thank you very much, Carmen. And I swear I'm not being negative, just honest. You are dealing here with a woman whose idea of strength training is lifting a fork three times a day. The whole concept of "vaginal appliances," as you call these gizmos, is simply unacceptable. I'm never going to use one. But of course, I said that about the dishwasher, answering machine, microwave, cash machine, computer, and cell phone, and now I couldn't get along without any of these. So I won't say never, just not now.

What is on my mind right now are my parents who live in Charleston and my daughter who lives in Seattle. I wish we could all be together for Thanksgiving, but it isn't going to happen this year.

Another thing on my mind now is my weight. The approaching holiday season has me neurosing about it. I've been gaining steadily for several years. Even with nocturnal yoga sessions

141

and relatively moderate eating (thank God none of you will ever see me to know how I lie), I can't seem to lose even a few pounds. Is it true that we gain seven pounds for every seven years after thirty-five? Does estrogen replacement therapy make it easier to lose weight? I wear a size sixteen now. Only a few years ago I was a twelve. Help and happy Thanksgiving!

The holiday weekend was a high-speed blur. When I got home from work the day before Thanksgiving, Mark was in the kitchen emptying bags of groceries. I was glad to have him back home, even for just a few days. Soon Sol came in with a pizza from Benny Tudino's. It's our custom on the eve of any holiday, when preparations are under way, to have pizza from Benny's and beer for supper. Sol and I have even been known to follow these casual meals with ice cream, an excess that we rationalize in the name of "making room in the freezer."

"You're going out? It's the night before Thanksgiving! Where could you possibly be going?" Mark was sputtering with surprise and maybe, I thought, a little disappointment.

I hid a smile. How often had I uttered those very same words to my son? On the first night of every vacation from college, Mark had no sooner arrived and wolfed down dinner than he was off for a reunion with old friends, a holiday party, or a club. Sol winked at me, signaling that he too appreciated the irony of tonight's role reversal.

"Betty wants to talk to Illuminada and me before the weekend, so we're meeting for coffee at the RIP. I shouldn't be long, an hour maybe." As I headed out the door, I called over my shoulder. "I don't see any flowers or wine. On my way home, I'll stop for some. That should save one of us a trip in the morning."

As soon as I got to the RIP, I noted Betty's smug I-know-something-you-don't-know grin. She didn't keep us in suspense long though. "Last Sunday after Mass when Father Santos asked me if I wanted to 'do lunch,' I knew something was up," she began.

"Father Santos?" I intoned. "Of course. I forgot all about him. What did he want?"

"He's very close to Altagracia's family. He's been helping Javier cope with Andreas. The poor kid has been acting out all over the place. And Javier himself is hardly any better." For a moment Betty's voice lowered. Then brightening, she continued, "But that's not why he wanted to talk to me. I've told him a little about our work, and . . ." Now the slow, deliberate pacing of Betty's words became infuriating.

"*Caramba!* Betty, I have to help my mother with Thanksgiving preparations. She insists on making all the Cuban dishes and all the American ones too. It's like an orgy at our house." Illuminada glanced at her watch. "And Luz will be getting off the train soon. No games." Illuminada pounded her small fist on the table in a mock threatening gesture, a good-humored effort to get Betty to speed up her narration.

"Okay. Sorry. I met Father Santos yesterday for lunch, and he told me about a certain family that belongs to his church. This is an old family that used to own a lot of property in town and that was once very, very powerful and influential politically. In the late eighties, they lost most of their money, and for the last few years the patriarch has been ill, seriously ill."

"Go on," Illuminada practically shouted. "So?"

"So," Betty continued, speaking in her usual deliberate way, "so the invalid gradually sold off everything but one piece of commercial property that he couldn't get rid of, a dilapidated old flophouse near here. A few years ago, just before Altagracia took over, he leased it to RECC to use as a Student Activities Center. The income from that lease has been helping to sustain him and his wife and her sister."

I tried to fit this news in the context of the crime we were struggling to solve. "So?" Illuminada repeated, impatience and frustration now sharpening her tone.

"So, Ms. Private Investigator," retorted Betty, "remember how I told you Altagracia tried to break that lease? Father Santos didn't even have to tell me the name of the family. We know from our files. It's old man Dworkin. So," she repeated, this time triumphantly, "all the leases were coming up for renewal. Altagracia would never have renewed that one. You've seen the place. It's just waiting for a Dumpster to come along so it can fall in. And yet the board approved that renewal last month along with all the others. Father Santos was, without exactly saying so, suggesting a motive."

"Yes, but Dworkin wasn't even at the festival, was he?" I queried. I found myself once again struggling to remember something, but as usual lately, my brain would not cooperate. I tried to relax, hoping that eventually this particular memory would emerge. Ruefully, I thought of how my past used to be instantly accessible, my mind a storehouse of useful data, filed neatly away, available at a moment's notice. Betty's voice brought me back to the conversation.

"No, but he's been around long enough and been big enough so that he wouldn't have had to be there. Lots of people owe him." Betty sipped her coffee and smiled, pleased with her latest contribution to our project.

"So, Sherlock, what you want me to do is check out the Dworkin connection, the family, right?" asked Illuminada, gathering her coat and briefcase and leaving a single and some change on the table. "If I agree, can I be excused now?" She saluted playfully, her good humor restored at the prospect of release. Halfway to the door, she turned around and came back to the table. "*Dios mio!* I almost forgot. Bel, you said you were going to Scottsdale this weekend? To that conference?"

"Yes. I'm presenting. You want me to bring you something? I hear the Native American jewelry is gorgeous." I was hoping to do a little shopping, perhaps on Saturday afternoon after my presentation.

"I want you to call your former colleague George Morgan. Remember? The hombre with the two teaching gigs? The one who's teaching out West now? From the files, you remember." Illuminada sounded impatient again.

"Okay. Got it. What about George? Let me guess. You want me to call him or meet with him and pump him about Dr. G, right?"

"*Si, senora.* Give him a call since from what I can gather, you're going to be in his barrio. Adios for real now. I'm outta here."

After Illuminada left, I sat with Betty for a few minutes until she finished her coffee and said, "Well, I've got to go too. I've invited Javier and Andreas and Javier's mother to have Thanksgiving dinner with me and Randy and my sister and her family. My sister's doing the turkey this year, but there's still plenty for me to do. I hope Randy isn't out late tonight. I'm not used to worrying about him driving or whatever since he's been away." I nodded, remembering the special anguish of waiting up for a teen.

Betty and I separated in the parking lot, and when I got in my car, I saw the Post-it on the dashboard reminding me to stop for flowers and wine. Happily the package store and florist are in the same mini mall. Both were bustling with other last-minute holiday shoppers. At the florist, I selected some gourds of different shapes and colors and two large bouquets of gigantic yellow chrysanthemums.

Carrying a shopping bag of gourds, I dashed into the package store behind my big and slightly unwieldy bouquets. Just inside, I collided with a man examining a bottle of wine. "Excuse me. I'm so sorry," I stammered, peering around my armful of flowers at the human obstacle in my path.

"Can I give you a hand with some of that, Professor Barrett?" The voice was familiar. I was face to face with Commissioner Tom Koladnar, who had put down the wine bottle and was taking my shopping bag off my arm as he spoke.

"Oh, hi. No, that's okay. I can manage." I tried to retain my hold on the bag, but he had already wrested it from me and placed it on the counter.

Smiling and winking at the clerk, he said, "Jerry, can Professor Barrett leave her packages here while she shops?" Flustered as always by the commissioner's solicitude, I surrendered my flowers. "Tell me, Professor, how are things going at RECC now? With the acting president and all? That was a terrible shock, a tragedy really. I hope it won't affect the governor's decision to provide some capital funding next year. Dr. Garcia and I worked so hard on that proposal. She was a real firebrand, you know. Not everybody's idea of a college president, but a real firebrand." He lowered his head for a moment, sighed, and then, looking straight into my eyes, said,

"Forgive me. Let's talk of brighter things. Will your family be home for this holiday?"

"My son will, but not my daughter. She won't get enough time off from work or classes," I answered dejectedly. Then as if in response to the younger man's consideration, I heard my own voice mouthing a total non sequitur. "Commissioner, I'm really worried about Oscar Beckman. He was one of my students, and I just can't imagine that boy poisoning Dr. Garcia. I wrote him a character reference, but I talked to his lawyer and even she thinks Oscar's chances of an acquittal are pretty slim." During this chance encounter, I found myself hoping that, as easily as Koladnar had relieved me of my packages, he might also ease my mind about Oscar.

Unable to stop myself, I babbled on, "Did you know that Oscar wrote and illustrated a children's cookbook as a project in one of his classes? There's a chance it might be published. He's talented . . ."

"So is O. J Simpson, Professor," the commissioner added curtly. In a tone of wry mockery, he went on, "You know, you English professors would forgive the devil himself if he could write a decent paragraph." Pausing a moment, he then continued gravely, "My problem is I just keep picturing that poor woman on the floor gasping for breath, writhing in agony. I will carry that memory with me until the day I die. I think, too, about Dr. Garcia's family, her own boy, motherless now, and her husband." He lowered his head for just a moment before continuing in a more businesslike tone, "But what makes you think Beckman didn't do it? As I recall, there's a lot of evidence against him. Do you suspect someone else?"

"Oh no," I replied quickly. "I guess having a boy around his age myself and all, I mean, I just . . ." I was absolutely blithering now, so I apologized, "Forgive me. I don't know what came over me. Now I really have to pick up some wine and get home. There's still so much to do. Happy holiday to you and your family." The ever gallant young man insisted on carrying my wine and flowers to my car and loading them into the hatchback for me.

On the short drive home, I reflected on my latest encounter with Tom Koladnar. Something about it bothered me, but I couldn't pinpoint what. I suddenly envisioned the memorial service for Dr. Garcia. Once more I heard Father Santos incanting the Lord's Prayer and saw the priest's eyes darting behind him in the direction of the dignitaries assembled on the stage. It was Father Santos's quick backward glance that I had tried without success to recall earlier that evening at the RIP. I was shivering as I pulled into my parking space.

Chapter 20

To: Menopausesupportgroup@powersurge.net
Subject: Depression
Date: Thurs, 24 Nov 1994 17:12:48
From: Bbarrett@circle.com

If I didn't know myself better, I'd say I was depressed. I am so tired. Right in the middle of a really pleasant Thanksgiving dinner, I just wanted to excuse myself and go to sleep. I felt so exhausted and depleted. And I didn't even cook this year.

Tomorrow I'm flying to Arizona for a national conference of community college faculty. I've prepared a solid three-hour workshop, and I usually enjoy making presentations. Since I've never been to a posh desert resort before, I was really looking forward to Scottsdale. Instead of buying a new bathing suit (oh God, do I have to?), and getting a decent haircut (why is my hair so thin now?), I worked until late last night. And of course, I can't sleep tonight. (No, Mitzi, don't tell me to do yoga.- I'm too wired and tired to do yoga.)

In spite of the allure of the desert, and all the preparation I've done, if it weren't that RECC has already paid my registration and airfare, I'd go visit my folks in Charleston or, perish the thought, just stay home. Imagine having hot flashes in the desert? Do I really need to be any dryer than I am? Do I need jet lag on top of my regular lag? How long will this go on? And what comes next?

Hurrying toward my car, I groped for the keys in my purse. Damn, where were they? I arrived at my Toyota breathless, fumbling frantically in my bag. Suddenly I sensed someone at my side, something hard prodding my back, an oddly familiar voice saying, "Give me the keys or—" I broke out in a sweat and began to scream, "No! Help! No!"

"Jesus, Bel, wake up! It's okay!" Sol's voice was urgent. As he shook my shoulder, he added, "It's okay if you don't want to. We don't have to. Jesus. It just seemed like a good idea at the time, that's all. But you've been having some nightmare. Want to tell Uncle Sol about it?"

As I gradually awakened, I was muttering and pushing away the bedclothes. "How did he know which car was mine? He's never seen my car."

"Easy, Bel," Sol was patting my arm and fanning my sweat-soaked body with a magazine. "Take it easy, love. Who's never seen your car?"

"Koladnar. Yet when he was helping me with the flowers and wine, the other night, he went right to it. I mean, he led the way. There were lots of other cars in that lot, but he looked around, and before I could say anything, he headed straight to mine. I didn't think anything of it until now after this dream . . ."

Sol was surprisingly reassuring. "Hey, Bel, you should know that your Toyota and my Beetle are usually the only nonluxury vehicles in that lot. That upscale mini mall's the easiest place for the folks en route to their gated palazzos in the outer burbs to pick up their dry cleaning and emergency rations of sushi and Chardonnay. They all drive Benzes and BMWs. Even their kids drive Saabs. Your little beat-up Bel-mobile stands out like a smile at a funeral in that crowd. It screams, 'My owner is an underpaid, un-appreciated academic slaving among the philistines' loud and clear. Haven't you ever noticed?"

Sol keeps forgetting I don't do cars. I mean, I drive one, but I don't pay much attention to what other people drive, so, of course, I'd been oblivious to how conspicuously outclassed my car was. Sol's reasoned words soothed me as, exhausted and still jet lagged after my return from Arizona, I got ready to face yet another day.

And it was quite a day. Quite a night actually. That evening at Betty's house we found out that our whole "investigation" was probably way off base. Let's face it. In a sense up until then we were totally clueless. I mean literally. Then all of a sudden we had a very plausible suspect. I wasn't real happy about it, but that's neither here nor there. The important thing was that we might very well be able to convince the cops that it was Linda Allen, not Oscar Beckman, who poi-soned Dr. G.

The evening started out really low key. It was the first meeting of our triumvirate after the Thanksgiv-ing holidays, so there was lots of chit-chat as we sprawled in Betty's living room sipping mulled wine surrounded by boxes of Christmas tree ornaments. Leave it to Betty. While the rest of us were still eating leftover Thanksgiving turkey, she was creating the perfect Christmas tree and serving holiday beverages à la Martha Stewart.

Betty sounded triumphant as she updated us on Randy. "Randy went back to Michigan." She raised both thumbs and grinned. "And he went without putting up a fuss. In fact, now he wants to spend part of Christmas at his roommate's in Detroit. And Tanisha, his girlfriend, says Randy and some other kids are cooking a little in the dorm. He doesn't talk much about his grades, but he studied some while he was here. I think he's adjusting. Lord, am I glad I didn't bring that dude home. You two were right on." Betty raised her glass to us. "How's Luz doing?"

"She still can't stand her roommate, but she got a work-study job in the library and that seems to be helping. She's met some other kids who work there. I know she's already worried about who to room with next year. But her grades are improving and she's real happy about that. *Caramba!* The kid's so driven." Illuminada sighed. Then she turned to me, "So how was the conference?"

With no freshman angst to report on, I'd been feeling a little out of the loop, so I was grateful to Illuminada for including me in their holiday reprise. "Actually, I'm glad I went. My presentation was well received. I really enjoyed the give and take. In fact, I'm thinking of going to graduate school."

"Sure. In your spare time. Tell us, is Scottsdale as spectacular as everybody says?" asked Betty.

"Better. The air is clean and dry and smells of blossoms, and the desert is lovely. Imagine me in a hot tub with two really attractive guys at night looking up at the stars, sipping a Pacifica, and talking about . . . nontraditional students and nonstandard dialects." I accompanied these last words with a grin of my own. "So how was your Thanksgiving with the Garcias?" I asked Betty.

"It was amazing. Randy was really good with Andreas. In fact, the two of them did all the dishes, even that big mother roasting pan. And then they went together to visit Randy's dad for an hour or so." I have to admire the calm and reasonable way Betty always talks about Randy's dad. You'd never know that he broke her heart when he left shortly after Randy turned ten. "Randy even invited Andreas to spend a weekend at the university next semester. Javier seemed pleased." Here Betty smiled.

Her smile faded as she continued, "But you know, now I'm even more worried about Javier than Andreas. He seems so agitated, almost manic. I decided to tell him that we three didn't buy the Oscar Beckman story and were trying to figure out who really poisoned Altagracia. I thought it might make him feel better and also that he might know something, remember something, that would be helpful. I even told him we were getting together here tonight and invited him to stop by. I'm not sure he will, but I thought it might help him to talk about her. I hope you two don't mind."

"No. I'm glad we'll get a chance to talk to him. I didn't want to bother him just yet, but we would have had to ask him some questions sooner or later." Illuminada sounded tired and resigned. Then she lightened up and said to Betty, "I suppose you got all your Christmas shopping done on Friday?"

"Actually, no. I did that last summer. But I wrapped everything." Betty's last words were barely audible over our collective groans in the face of her practically obsessive efficiency.

"You know," interjected Illuminada, focused again, "I saw Javier the night before Thanksgiving. Near the RIP, on the corner there. I recognized him from the memorial service. I wanted to go over to him and say something, you know, express condolences or something like that, but I don't really know him, so I felt a little funny. Anyway, he looked like he was having an argument with a young woman, a student maybe. Doesn't he teach painting at State?" Illuminada helped herself to a handful of popcorn.

Betty answered quickly, "Yes. He's doing a year there as artist in residence." Then Betty turned businesslike, asking, "So are we going to get down, or what? Where do we stand now? Illuminada, did you find out anything about Dworkin?"

"Only that it's true what Father Santos told you. The old man's been ill, and the rent he gets from RECC is practically the family's sole means of support. He has a tiny pension and Social Security, but they're not enough for them all to live on now that he's so sick. One of his nurses is a current client of mine, and I got her to talking and she just happened to mention that Dworkin has a son, Marv. Marv's an out-of-work sales rep, who visits occasionally. Marv told her he's applying for a job at—"

"Oh no," I burst in. "Let me guess. He's applying for an administrative slot at RECC, right? Wendy told me this morning that there were six, count them, six assistant dean and/or director slots advertised in yesterday's paper. Dr. G had eliminated all those extraneous administrative slots, remember, Betty?" I didn't wait for Betty to nod before I went on, "She was going to try to hire a few more full-time faculty instead. That's what the last accrediting team recommended."

"Well adios full-time faculty slots and *buenvenidos* Marv Dworkin," replied Illuminada. "I'm waiting for the results of one more search on that family. Things were a little slow because of the holidays. But it's easy to see why Dworkin would want Altagracia out of the way. It's just hard to see how he or Marv either, for that matter, was in a position to do anything about it."

Shifting our focus, Iluminada turned toward me and asked, "And what did you learn about George Morgan? He comes up clean in my book."

"Yeah, I talked to him. He was at the conference, so it was easy. He told me his wife has lupus and can't work steadily. In fact, she often needs some help at home. They have three kids. They couldn't make it on just the forty grand he earned at RECC. When Dr. G gave him an ultimatum that would have forced him to give up his full-time faculty job at NJIT, he gave up both teaching jobs. He took a position teaching business at the Community College of Pueblo Vista, Arizona which pays him almost as much as the two New Jersey positions put together, and he teaches only twelve credits a semester there. At RECC we teach fifteen. He relocated his family to Pueblo Vista. There is no way George Morgan killed Dr. G. In fact, he said he was grateful to her because now his work-load is halved, and the whole family loves Pueblo Vista."

Betty was the first to speak. "So we cross him off our list. This is discouraging. In spite of the fact that Dworkin's lease is continued and his son will proba-bly get a good job and Tarantello's nephew is now on the payroll, and Danzig got a huge raise, the only one there is any hard evidence against is still Oscar Beck-man."

I decided to put in my two cents. There was little to lose. "You know, I ran into Commissioner Kolad-nar Wednesday night after I left you two, and I told him how worried I was about Oscar. He wasn't very sympathetic."

"Give us a few details, Bel," directed Illuminada,

reaching for another handful of popcorn. So I filled them in on my chance encounter with Koladnar in the wine store.

"Lord, girl, the dude was nice to you, but you're making him sound sort of sinister," Betty commented after I described how the commissioner had carried my purchases to my car.

I smirked, saying, "Remember, he's a career politician." Then I continued in a serious voice, "Don't laugh, but I had another nightmare, and he was in it, his voice, I mean. I remembered something that may just be very important." I recounted my dream. Then to be fair, I also explained Sol's interpretation of events. "What do you two think? I mean, could it be that Koladnar knew what kind of car I drive because he tampered with my brakes or had somebody else tamper with them?"

Betty paused thoughtfully before she spoke, "The problem with him as a suspect is that Altagracia's death doesn't seem to have made any difference to him, you know? He's in good shape regardless. He gets reelected every term. But . . ."

"The search I'm waiting for may tell us something about him. I should have thought of this before. Maybe he's too good to be true," added Illuminada, pushing the popcorn bowl away. "*Como mierda*! Take this please," she begged. "Do you know I've gained three pounds since we started getting together?"

Betty and I feigned shock as we placed the bowl between us on the sofa. "We wouldn't want you to break a hundred, girl," said Betty scathingly.

"Right," I quipped. "You might not be able to shop in the children's section anymore."

"Bitch, bitch, bitch. if you don't mind focusing for just one minute more on the matter at hand, I think one of you should find a reason to chat with Tarantello. He's the only suspect we haven't had face-to-face contact with. We have nothing to lose but a little time."

"You're right," I said. "I suppose I can go to him as a representative of the memorial committee. Heaven knows, I don't have much time so near the end of the semester, but I'll try to talk to him early next week."

"Good. By then my computer searches will be done. Now, Bel," said Illuminada, "are you still mentoring me through my first semester as an adjunct? Because I want you to help me make up a final exam and a way to help them review for it. Any ideas?"

"Yo! Don't get her started on that," Betty rolled her eyes in mock horror at the prospect of listening to me talk about the classroom. Just then, the doorbell chimed, and when Betty answered it, there stood Javier Garcia.

# Chapter 21

November 25, 1994

Dear Professor Barrett,

I am write to say I thank you for invitation to your house to celebrate American festival which is the Thanksgiving. Now I understand much better about this holiday. Especially the food was very delicious even though I do not eat turkey bird or sea creatures baked in milk. You know in my religion we eat vegetarians. I was enjoying many new foods at your feast, especially the pecan pie and what you call turnips. For me it was interesting that the food have no spices in it. I am glad that everybody enjoy the dessert I bring made from crispy rice. I have interest also that in America the men prepare and offer holiday meal. Even they clean dishes.

Everybody of your guests was nice with me about my english which still not very good. Your son mark especially was nice with me listening to me slowly with good ears. I understand a lot of talking at your house.

I see you were crying after you speak on telephone with your daughter. The other people they did not see you, but

I see you. I hope she is not sick or with problems so far away on this important American holiday. You look sad also after your father telephone from Charleston. I am sad you feel sad.

But your house is very beautiful. So many ornaments to look at. So many books. It was nice when your friend Sol play the piano too. The piano is expensive I know so that is why you have no tv. I hope someday you can get tv. Sol play music very good and he cook good. He have nice daughter alexis, who very respectful to her parents. I hope Alexis finish her studies before her baby come. Alexis boyfriend from China, but he speak good English, not like me. It was interesting that Sols wife from his divorce is there with her very new husband. She nice, but not like you. And Sols mother is nice too. She like a sexy movie star in that mini skirt and with big earrings that shine. In my country, double grandmothers are very old ladies. I like Sols mothers boyfriend (is that word correct?), even though he is much younger for her. In America do men like women older?

My uncle say American Thanksgiving festival is about football, but now I know he is wrong. Now with your kindness I know how Thanksgiving really is about in a true American family.

Your student,
Rheka Patel

Javier had been drinking. For days maybe. The one other time I'd met Javier he'd been very well groomed. Now his long dark hair hung in unkempt strings, his denim jacket was stained, his shirt rumpled, and his eyes glazed. To complete the effect, he reeked of wine and cigarettes. But even so, I had to acknowledge that he was still an attractive man. He and Altagracia had made a glamourous twosome.

Taking in his condition, Betty led Javier to a chair, and I got him some coffee from the pot in the kitchen. He gulped the coffee and nodded as Betty made introductions.

To give Javier time to collect himself, Betty kept talking. She directed her words to Illuminada and me, but she spoke slowly, as if in the presence of a child. "After Thanksgiving dinner while the boys were doing the dishes and Altagracia's mom was having a little rest, Javier and I went for a walk around the block, you know the usual walk-off-the-turkey-before-we-orgy-out-on-pie stroll. I wanted to find out how the bereavement group that Father Santos had found for Andreas was going. Well, like I said, I told Javier about our project, and he promised he'd stop by tonight."

Javier's eyes kept moving toward the door. I expected him to bolt any second. He started to speak. His voice was almost expressionless, at odds with his dramatic entrance and trapped demeanor. "You know what really gets me is she'd hate this. She'd hate having anybody, even you, Betty, know our personal business. But I've got to talk to you. Because Linda may just be the one you're looking for. You know that, don't you? Little Linda, she could just be the one. Okay, here goes."

Javier inhaled and continued in the same monotone, "Early last summer when Altagracia was spending so much time on campus drafting the college's five-year plan or whatever the hell she was doing, I made a big mistake." Now Javier cradled his head in his hands and directed his muffled words at the floor. "There's this graduate student Linda, Linda Allen. A very talented girl. I was helping her put together a portfolio for a fellowship application. I gave her a lot of time and attention. She started wanting more." Javier took another swig of coffee. When he continued, he was sitting up, his eyes on the ceiling.

"To be honest, I was feeling neglected." Javier shook his head back and forth as if to acknowledge the absurdity of his excuses. He forced himself to go on. "After Altagracia became president of RECC, she didn't pay very much attention to me. Now don't get me wrong. I'd always supported her ambition. That's what attracted me to her when we met, her energy and drive, that incredible will to succeed." He paused a moment, shaking his head again, this time as if to ward off a memory.

"But after she'd achieved her goal and become a college president before she was forty, things between us started changing. She was just never home. Even Andreas noticed that she wasn't around much." At the mention of his son's name, Javier reburied his head in his hands and rubbed his eyes before continuing.

"So by now, *senoras,* you can figure out what I did, right? Of course you can. I had a little thing with Linda. We'd meet at my studio. Now don't get me wrong. I told the kid right up front it was no big thing, that I loved my wife, that this was just a feel-good-now kind of deal for me. I was flattered..." Now Javier stood up and began pacing back and forth across Betty's living room while the three of us tried to follow what he was saying.

"Somehow Altagracia found out." He smiled a rueful smile, more like a grimace really. "She was always too smart for her own good. Now don't get me wrong. I guess I wanted her to know in a way, so she'd see how much I needed her. Sounds crazy now, doesn't it?" He stopped pacing and looked at us for

the first time since he had arrived. "Anyway, Linda
had started calling me at home, and a couple of times
I stayed at the studio later than usual, whatever. Anyway, Altagracia confronted me and threatened to
leave me if I continued to see Linda. She said I had
to tell Linda it was over and stick to it. I had absolutely no problem with that. Linda was nothing to me.
It was always Altagracia. And believe it or not, I'd
never done anything like this before. Besides, Linda's
a student. Now don't get me wrong. I'm not really
the kind of guy who makes it with students, you
know? I hate guys like that." Javier paused, forcing
the fingers of both hands through his matted hair.

"So I told Linda it was over. And then my real
problems began. Linda didn't seem to believe me. She
started following me around, almost like in that
movie. Man, like she was stalking me. She left notes
on my car, hung out around my office at State, waited
outside my studio. She even started following me
home at night. I was terrified. I was afraid Andreas
would run into her. I was even afraid she'd harm herself somehow. After all, she's just a kid. And I
couldn't go to anyone at the university." Now Javier's
voice was harsh with self-deprecation.

"Well, I was at the goddamn Fall Festival. You
know." He nodded in Betty's direction. "I assembled
and hung all the art for that. Of course, Linda had
followed me around there too. Wherever I went, she
would turn up, like a shadow. And you know the
rest." Javier collapsed into his chair, leaned back, and
closed his eyes.

To our surprise he continued to speak. "You see my
problem, you smart *profesores*? If I keep quiet about
this and it turns out that Linda's guilty, Linda goes
free and can continue to torment me and poison any-

body else who gets in her way. And the Beckman kid goes to jail. But by going public about Linda, I give my son the chance to see how his no-good *papi* caused his mother's death because he couldn't keep it in his pants."

And so we had a whole new scenario to consider, and I, for one, didn't like it. Instead of saving Oscar Beckman and RECC from the ravages of greedy and corrupt bureaucrats, we were confronted with the Joey Buttafucco of the local art scene and yet another deluded Amy Fisher, as pathetic in her pathology as anyone who ever killed for love. The possibility that Dr. G had died as the result of this tabloid-type triangle moved her death from the realm of tragedy to that of senseless tragedy.

"Betty, I'm going outside for a smoke." So saying, Javier was out the door, leaving us to digest his story. Betty was choking back tears. "I can't stand it that she spent the last few months of her short life suffering on account of that sorry-assed doofus." She gestured toward the door. "And what about Andreas? Javier's right, damn him. How can the boy live with this? He worshipped his mother and he adores his dad. Who will he be left with after this? What will this do to him?" I sat next to Betty on the sofa, pulled her over to me, and held her while Illuminada and I talked.

Illuminada looked at me hard, saying, "Bel, I know you don't like this either, but let's deal with it. *Dios mio*, this is not like a book where if you don't like the way the story is going you just put it down. And that goes double for you, Betty. *Como mierda!* You think Dr. Garcia would want this Linda wandering around loose? Who knows what she might still do to Javier? To Andreas even?"

I was grateful for Illuminada's insight and her

sharp, practical words recalling me to the problem at hand. We had to finish what I, in fact, had started.

"Okay. If Javier comes back, let's find out as much as we can about Linda Allen." Frankly, I doubted Javier would come back. After all, having dumped his sordid little saga in our laps, maybe he felt now his problem was our problem, so we'd solve it for him without the need for further involvement or embarrassment on his part. And talking to us had to be embarrassing for him, especially as he sobered up.

So I was surprised when the door opened and Javier walked back in engulfed in a cloud of smoke, looking a little like the devil in an amateur production of *Faust* and smelling like him too. Betty blew her nose, settled her laptop on her knees, and opened it.

"Javier," she began, "where were you when Altagracia collapsed? I don't remember you working the crowd with us."

"No." Javier looked down at his cowboy boots. "I was way across the terminal hustling paintings. You know, I had a lot of my own stuff hanging. The Fall Festival was great exposure, and it's been a while since I've had a show. Now don't get me wrong, but Altagracia didn't need me to work the crowd, and there was some interest in my own work from a restaurant owner. I was talking to him about one of my murals. He wanted it for over his bar. He was going to bid."

"So," Illuminada said, "was Linda with you or could she have been over near Betty and your wife? Do you recall?" Illuminada was leaning forward in her chair, waiting for his reply.

"No. She wasn't with me, but I don't know where she was. Andreas was with me though. Linda had hung some of her own work, and then she came over and asked if she could help install mine. I told her no. I took her aside and told her to leave the area where I was, to stop harassing me. I apologized again for hurting her and told her once more that I loved my wife and son. She was crying when she walked away. I don't know where she went after that. The next thing I knew, Altagracia was on the floor." Javier grimaced as he said those words.

"Do you have a picture of Linda?" It had occurred to me that a photo might be useful in trying to place Linda at the time of the murder.

"We also need Linda's address, her age, the names of her friends, roommates, everything you can think of about her. Is she a full-time student or does she work? Who's her adviser?" Illuminada was weighing in now. "Does she have any old boyfriends? Did she get the fellowship you were helping her with? What sort of art does she do? Has she ever been to the State counseling department?" Illuminada fired questions at Javier and, to the best of his ability, he answered them. But he didn't know too much about the girl. As he put it, "Don't get me wrong, but we talked mostly about art, about colors, about style and technique. Then later on, after I told her it was over, we just started arguing and . . . you know." He shrugged.

Finally Betty said, "Javier, why not go home and try to get some rest? I'll call you when we need to talk to you again. Maybe you'll think of something else when your head is clearer. Go now." She didn't even stand to show him out, but gestured dismissively with her head in the direction of the door.

Illuminada cautioned his retreating figure, "Don't say anything to anybody. Give us a few days." And with that Javier left. To Betty and me, Illuminada said,

"I still have a few friends at State, so I'll see what I can dig up."

"Mark's best friend from high school, Luke Benjamin, is studying metal sculpting at State. Maybe he can get us some information," I volunteered, not at all sure how cooperative Mark would be given his antipathy to even the idea of my involvement in this case. I might have to contact Luke myself. "But in the meantime, I'm still going to check out Tarantello as planned. I just can't put what Wendy told me about his nephew's résumé out of my head completely."

Chapter 22

To Menopausesupportgroup@powersurge.com
Subject: HRT or not
Date: Sun, 4 Dec 1994 03:08:52
From: Bbarrett@circle.com

I wish these researchers would make up their minds. I mean, what is the deal with this hormone replacement therapy? One day I pick up the paper and read that estrogen is the panacea. A pill a day will save me from strokes and bone loss. And if I take two different hormone pills a day, as a bonus, I can increase my chances of avoiding uterine and colon cancer as well. Neato. The next day I pick up the paper and read how if I take these pills, my breasts become a "danger zone," like my mother's did. The percentages they throw around are mind-boggling. What do they mean?

I have an appointment with a new doctor next week (what fun, back in the stirrups again). I got her name from the list Sandra e-mailed me (thank you again, Sandra.) I plan to try to get some answers. I hope I like her. Just once I'd like to walk into a gyno's waiting room and find an old *Lears* or even a copy of *Modern Maturity* and pamphlets on HRT and hot flashes on the rack alongside all the literature on parenting and breast feeding.

After Javier's revelation, my meeting with RECC board president Dominic Tarantello was anticlimactic at best. It had been easy to get an appointment with him at his suite of offices in the gleaming new Jersey City Sewage and Water Authority Tower. The Board of Commissioners, who had appointed him to RECC's Board of Trustees, had justified its decision by citing his executive experience as director of JCSWA. However, this executive experience had not sufficed to stem the rising cost of water and sewage disposal in Jersey City. "Good morning, Mr. Tarantello. Thank you for seeing me. As I told your secretary, I'm here on behalf of the RECC Student Government's Altagracia Garcia Memorial Committee."

Tarentello smiled and motioned me to sit down. "Good morning, Professor Barrett. Fine morning. It's always a pleasure to be of service, to assist the students of RECC. What can I do? What service can I render?" Tarantello smiled at me again across his massive desk.

Amused as usual by the sewage mogul's "double-talk," I felt a giggle coming on. Opening my fan, I took refuge behind it while I explained my errand.

"A scholarship would seem to be one thing. It would seem to be a particular item. A plaque is another. A plaque is quite different from a scholarship," he reiterated. Closing his eyes and furrowing his brow, Tarantello appeared to be pondering these options.

"Yes, I quite agree," I contributed maliciously. I was relishing his discomfort. I moved my fan forward and back, waiting for the sewage czar to draw some sort of inference from the data.

He surprised me by posing a question. "What have others, people besides me, had to say on this matter? The matter of the plaque or the scholarship?"

"Well, I don't know about the students, but the administrators I've talked to favor a plaque, and the faculty, of course, favor a scholarship," I answered.

"I see. I understand. Well, that settles and decides it. I favor and support a plaque. I'm sure, that is, I'm certain, that my fellow board members, my colleagues on the board, will agree. Is there anything else, anything further? I'm always happy to give my opinion, provide input."

"I'm looking forward to meeting your nephew, our new director of the Career Development Center. He must be quite something to have beaten out all the competition. It will be wonderful for our students to have the benefit of his wisdom and experience." As I uttered this blatant lie, I focused on Tarantello's expression.

I was taken aback when his features relaxed into a huge grin. He said, "Yes. Frankie's a good man, a fine person. He's well qualified with good credentials. He'll do an excellent job. He'll perform very well." Tarantello stood.

I stood too and, refusing a tour of the sewage treatment plant, left his office. I felt soiled, as if I had been somehow sullied by the proximity of so much sewage. I took deep breaths of the cold December air as I walked to my car. It was good to get back to my own office, cramped and cluttered though it was.

The bright yellow of Rheka's sari flared like a banner outside my door. I had been worried about her because she hadn't shown up for last Friday's ESL class. She was determined to set my mind at ease. "Sorry I miss our class on Friday," she began as I removed my coat. "My aunt she went to the airport to get my uncle. He come back from India. She want me to watch the baby so I not can go to school that day. Do not worry, Professor. I will make up all my work, I promise."

Rheka smiled her most ingratiating smile and went on, "We had big party that night with all delicious foods from my country. Many relatives and friends come to our house to welcome back my uncle. We work very hard to make food for this party. Sanjay come with his mother and his kid. His mother she look at me a lot while I was serving the food. She talk with my uncle a lot."

Suddenly Rheka turned shyly around in the tiny room, saying, "My uncle bring sari from my country. My parents they send it to me. And this also." She held up her thin arm to show me a bangle bracelet. "From my sister," Rheka added. She miss me. My parents they miss me too. I cry all night after this party. But I go now." And she was out the door before I could utter even a word.

Concepcion was on time for her appointment with me, but she seemed preoccuppied and frazzled. "Professor Barrett, I have to miss the rest of the semester," she began. I'm sure my dismay registered on my face, because she continued quickly, "I'm flying to Puerto Rico tonight. It's my grandmother. She's in the hospital again. Her diabetes and her heart keep acting up. Between her sugar and her pressure, it's a miracle she's still with us. Last semester I had to drop out to take care of her. But now we're so close to the end of the semester, my counselor says I should try to work out terms for an incomplete with my teachers."

"Oh Concepcion, I'm so sorry. You've been doing so well. Are you sure you can't wait until the end of the semester to leave?" I inquired rather lamely. I knew the answer.

"My grandmother took care of me all the time when I was small. She's like a second mother to me. Is it the paper that's the problem or the final?" Concepcion frowned now, trying to understand the opposition my question implied.

I persisted. "And what about your work? Can you get the time off there?"

"I'm taking off a month. My supervisor at the center doesn't like it because a lot of our clients go crazy from now until New Year's. People act out during these next few weeks. They'll have to divide up my caseload. I'll have to speak to my landlord too. But this is something I have to do."

I felt powerless in the face of Concepcion's determination. I hoped she would finish her coursework and return to school for the next semester. I knew how much she enjoyed college and how long she had waited to attend. We spent the next half hour going over a draft of her paper, and when she finally left, she promised to mail in the paper, her remaining reader responses, and the take-home final exam I handed her. Her paper had the germ of a fascinating discussion of the use of ghosts in Morrison's *Beloved* and *Macbeth*. I hoped she'd finish it.

As if sensing my doubt, Concepcion said, "You know I'll do my work, Professor Barrett. I always do. Besides, I owe it to the memory of Dr. Garcia to graduate. She died for this place, for people like me, so we could get an education."

And so having pledged her word to both me and the ghost of Dr. G, Concepcion gathered her books and walked out of my office, my "Safe journey" echoing down the hall after her.

 *Chapter 23*

To: Bbarrett@circle.com
Subject: Good News!
Date: Sun, 11 Dec 1994 16:15:48
From: Rbarrett@UWash.edu

Mom,

Thanks for the care package of Hanukkah surprises. I especially liked the purple socks and the membership in AAA and the M&M's. Keith loves the biking magazines. We did make latkes, but not too many. It's hard to grate all those potatoes. Keith really scarfed them up though. Maybe for next year we'll borrow a food processor. Would that work?

Anyway, guess what Sol's giving me and Keith for a "pan-holiday" gift? (I swear, Mom, that man is funny.) He made us plane reservations to come home as soon as I get out of school. We set it all up to coincide with Keith's vacation days which he has to use up anyway. They weren't too happy when I told them at work, but I gave plenty of notice. So don't freak when you see us. We'll be there in less than two weeks. Sol has the dates and times. He's meeting our flight because he says you don't finish with exams and preregistration until late on Friday, December 23, and Mark will be working until then too. I wish we could've surprised you, but I didn't want to get you all worked up at your age (only kidding). Besides, this way you'll cry now while you're reading this and you'll be over it by the time we actually arrive, right? Anyway, we all know I can't keep a secret.

Love you,
Rebecca, the Latke Queen

P. S. Speaking of secrets, Mark is all bent out of shape over your "investigation" of Dr. Garcia's death. He says you even asked him to ask Luke Benjamin about some girl in the Art Department at State. Mark thinks you're in "deep doo doo" and told me to talk you into letting the police handle it. I told him to chill because you know what you're doing. Do you?

I should be grateful that I didn't let a little stress and low-level depression get the best of me. At least I didn't let them keep me from my annual theater date with Sarah on Tuesday night. Every year Sarah gets free tickets to the holiday production of State's Drama Department, and she always asks me to accompany her. I usually look forward to this evening of dinner and theater with Sarah. But that morning I sat sipping tea in the kitchen rereading my horrific spring schedule, which had appeared in my mailbox the day before, and contemplating suicide.

I haven't had a schedule like that in years. A Friday night class and four eight o'clocks, including one on Saturday? There are a few adjuncts who always want those weekend classes because they have other work during the week. Why was Joe Fink, my department chair, giving them to me, a veteran of two decades at RECC? Especially after I updated all those course outlines for him last summer. I saved him a month's work. What was his problem? Damn.

All I wanted to do was crawl back into bed, pull the covers over my head, and stay there until summer. The December sunlight hitting the newspaper and vitamin bottles on the counter didn't warm me. "I wish I could get out of this damn theater date with Sarah tonight," I whined.

From the piano bench where Sol-the-morning-person was already learning a new Scarlatti sonata, he answered with that implacable logic I've always found so unreasonable, "So why don't you? By the way, let's try to make the Citizens' Committee to Preserve the Waterfront meeting next week, okay? We got a mailing about some new development project, a six-story addition, on River Street, 242 I think. Something about illegal permits and variances. Apparently the building's a real eyesore. Have you seen it?"

"No. I'll try to get by there after I turn in my final grades. I can't say about next week yet," I answered grumpily. "I'm still trying to get through today."

"Seriously, Bel, if you're beat, stay home tonight. I'll cook. Sarah will understand." Sol's voice was gentle.

I wasn't up to explaining why breaking a date with an old friend simply because I'm a little tired and suicidal was not an option. Instead I countered, "Thanks, but I'll probably feel better after classes, and the play is David Mamet's *Oleanna*. It's supposed to be really good. Right up my alley. It's been filmed, you know. And maybe it'll take my mind off all this other stuff." Sol returned his attention to Scarlatti. He knows how I always talk myself into doing things I'm ambivalent about.

But later, alone on the way to work, I faced facts. I was not only tired and angry but really discouraged. For two months Betty, Illuminada, and I had probed every angle of Dr. G's murder we could think of and we had come up with nothing. Zilch. Nada. Sure, lots of people, people like Nelson Danzig, Cesar Nuevos, Dominic Tarantello, Dwayne Smith, and, now, Linda Allen, had had motives, but no one, it seemed, except this Linda Allen, had also had both the method and the opportunity. If Linda had an alibi, Oscar Beckman's mother might be in treatment for a long time. I was imagining the reality of Oscar's jailtime when I arrived at RECC.

It didn't help my mood that my students were in the throes of their typical end-of-semester anxiety. Rheka was waiting at the door of my office. She was terrified about the basic skills tests she would have to take later in the week. Until she passed them, she couldn't take any college-level courses. She started chatting about the practice writing sample she'd done the day before while I was taking off my coat. "I know I fail that writing test for practice that you give us. Not enough time. Not enough words. And then I am so nervous even the words in English which I know I forget. What means 'terminally ill'? I wrote how one time I got sick in train terminal in my country. And with the reading test too, I fail. Not enough time. Not enough words. My uncle be mad with me. Thanks god I gonna pass calculus test with good grade. I am afraid to tell my uncle about my English. He expect me to be smart. He gonna think I am not learning."

And so it went throughout the day. One group was reviewing for exams. Another had requested conferences so they could go over final drafts of research papers. In my third class of the day, there were oral presentations. My students' stress is always palpable during oral presentations, especially when I tape them, and I always tape the final speeches. In the face of their quaking voices and trembling hands, I felt drained. I was relieved when my teaching day ended at three.

But at RECC the end of the teaching day seldom means the end of the workday. I had yet to endure a particularly insulting meeting of the Academic Council. This august body had been "reorganized" shortly after Dr. Garcia's murder, with the result that administrators now constituted the council's majority. Today they actually voted to increase the cap on class size from thirty to "whatever the room will hold." Lord Nelson himself had argued in favor of this travesty by saying, "More sailors will find ample berth on board our vessel. Increasing class size will provide recruits with more opportunities for interacting with those who navigate similar waters." By the end of the meeting, I found myself counting the minutes until I could desert this particular ship of fools to go meet Sarah. Besides, sometime between reviewing for finals and listening to poor speech phobic Damian Hotchkiss's attempt at a speech, I'd gotten an idea.

I arrived before Sarah at Laico's, an excellent Italian restaurant close to Jersey City State. The small dining room was festooned with holiday wreaths and tinsel. I claimed a table and asked our waiter to open the bottle of Soave I ordered. I downed a glass before Sarah came in. "Am I glad to see you," I heard myself say as Sarah bent over to brush my cheek with hers. And I really was.

"Pictures?" I knew that like all good grandmothers, Sarah would have a slew of recent photos of Hannah ready to whip out at the slightest show of interest. Sure enough, Sarah reached into her bag and pulled out an envelope of snapshots. There was Hannah sleeping, Hannah smiling, Hannah naked, Hannah in a lime green sleeper suit, Hannah in a car seat, and, of course, the obligatory one of Hannah in Sarah's lap. The baby was more adorable than ever now, a succulent six-month-old armful. My inner grandmother downed a big swig of Soave while I oohed and aahed appreciatively.

Only after carefully replacing the photos in her purse did Sarah say, "Let me catch up." She filled both of our wine glasses and remarked cheerfully, "Hey, I'm so glad we're doing this again. It's a nice break. And I sure need one. You look a little peaked yourself. Too many exams?"

I was soon complaining to Sarah, off the record, of course, about the dispiriting nonresults of our investigation. As we shared an order of fried calamari and then an arugula salad, I recounted the whole sordid saga, which really amounted to nothing at all. "But Sarah Wolf, education reporter par excellence, here's where you come in. Could you find a pretext for interviewing this Linda Allen? Then maybe you could establish where the hell she was when Dr. G was poisoned. It'd sure save me time and energy."

Sarah did not look surprised by my request. Instead she said, "I thought you'd never ask. Of course. I'll use the fellowship angle. She'll be thrilled with the exposure. Consider it done. And don't worry, I'll keep everything off the record until you give me the word. But Bel Barrett, I better be the first to know when you figure this out. I want to break the story."

"It's a deal," I told her. "But don't hold your breath."

"Bel, I know you're very worried about the Beckman kid, but it's not as if you have to resolve this by the end of the semester. These things take time. Just don't push it. Be careful. And don't let it make you crazy or completely subsume the holidays either. Is Rebecca coming home?"

Sarah's reminder that the rest of the world did not turn on the academic calendar got my attention. She was right. Out of unexamined habit I had been expecting to figure out by semester's end who had poisoned Dr. G. My zeal for closure had always been well served by the school year. Its ritualistic deadlines and finals contributed to the illusion that you could tie things up neatly every few months. I always turn in my final grades feeling that, for a while anyway, school is over. I'm free to read a novel unrelated to coursework, reorganize my closets, or contemplate a trip with a clear conscience until it's time to plan for the next semester. Seeing the murder investigation as a course in which I could get an incomplete was a relief in spite of the fact that Oscar Beckman's preliminary hearing was rapidly approaching. I felt grateful to Sarah for granting me this extension, so to speak, and raised my glass in her general direction to signify that I got her message.

Sarah had her own problems. She was angling for a richly deserved promotion, and we brainstormed strategies she could use to win it. Since I hadn't had time for more than a cold muffin and a banana all day, I really chowed down on the shoemakers' chicken and eggplant rollatini we shared. We also divvied up a slab of Gino's homemade tiramisu, laughing about our meeting in that long ago aerobics class. I wasn't surprised that we'd knocked off most of a second bottle of Soave by the time we left. Fortunately we only had to drive a few blocks.

More than a little mellow and full to bursting, we arrived at the theater about fifteen minutes before curtain time. Sarah had just recognized a long-lost cousin seated behind us when I realized that I'd forgotten to use the ladies' room at Laico's. I was furious with myself because I knew that the one at the theater would, as usual, be crowded. I'd have to stand in line with others who, like me, wouldn't be able to make it through the first act without a potty visit.

Sure enough, the predictable queue was there, at least twenty women long. At the front, near the rest room entrance, chatting women stood patiently, brightening visibly as the sound of each flush heralded the opening of a stall door. Toward the end of the line, those less fortunate waited stoically to advance to the front. Resigned, I took my place behind them and, suddenly very warm, began fanning myself.

The smartly dressed young woman in front of me was wearing perfume heavy with the cloying scent of gardenias. I sneezed, and instantly felt a familiar pressure. My grip on my fan tightened as I realized that I might not have time to wait on this line. I envisioned myself having to make excuses and flee the theater, smelly and wet. I glanced at the men's room. A man was just leaving. Wendy and I had commandeered empty men's rooms in theaters all over Manhattan, from the Mitzi Newhouse to the Lucille Lortel. One of us always stayed outside to hold off unwitting males eager to claim their territory.

I waited as long as I could to see if anyone else would emerge. When no one did, unable to sustain the pressure for another minute, I dashed for the

door. There was no one at the urinals. Quickly checking the view from the bottom of the stalls, I was relieved to see that none was occupied. Entering the
nearest cubicle, I dropped my purse to the floor,
yanked down my tights, and sat without even wiping
the seat, an unprecedented breach of custom for me.
I smiled as my bladder emptied. What luck to have
found the place deserted! In Manhattan the women
behind me would have followed my lead, but my Jersey City sisters did not.

In fact, I was just reaching for the toilet paper when
I heard the unmistakable burr of male voices and the
clang of the men's room door. Without thinking, I
grabbed my purse off the floor and raised my feet,
planting them on the door opposite the toilet. There I
sat, staring at my sensible brown suede T-straps, in-
congruous against a background of student-penned
obscenities. I found myself praying that my taupe
tights, now dangling beneath my suspended thighs,
and the skirt of my taupe silk dress, now bunched
around my ample middle, were not visible. I felt ridiculous and wondered briefly why I hadn't called
out to warn the men of my presence. After all, this
was the nineties, and we were all friends, weren't we?
Unisex bathrooms were de rigueur in lots of places.
The guys would have understood, wouldn't they?
But, a product of forties toilet training, I hadn't announced myself, and so there I was, accordion-pleated
into a men's room stall, undignified and, worse yet,
unwiped. I couldn't help but be amused by my pre-
dicament as I waited for them to do what they came
for and leave.

But suddenly my heart stopped, and I broke out in
a sweat. Over the sound of their combined streams
hitting the urinal, I recognized the voice of Tom Ko-

ladnar. It was unmistakable. And he was talking with Dominic Tarantello. I was sure of it. I made out the words "arrogant bitch" and "meddling busybody outsider . . ." I reached into the purse on my lap and groped until my fingers closed around my tape recorder. Moving slowly and, I prayed, silently, I pulled it out and pushed record. ". . . lease renewals went through with no problem, right? You got your nephew on the payroll, right? Nice kid, Frankie. Things will go back to normal now."

"Yeah normal, like usual, like they were before she came."

"Right. We've got a lot of other folks waiting too, local folks, who deserve a real crack at those new positions."

"Yeah, they earned the right. They deserve it."

"And we know how to thank Jenkins. He's easy. We know what will make him happy. It's good we . . ."

I thought I heard the faint metallic noise of a zipper but Tarantello was talking and I couldn't be sure. I could hardly make out his words over the pounding of my heart. Holding the tape recorder as close to the bottom of the stall as I could without exposing it, I tensed as the voices receded a little, and I heard footsteps on the tile. Then there was the sound of running water. They were washing their hands. Damn. Further conversation was muffled by the whooshing of the automatic hand dryer. When it ended, I heard footsteps again. I exhaled only when the closing of the door behind the two men cut off their voices.

"Welcome back. I was beginning to think you'd fallen in. You just made it," cracked Sarah as I squeezed through the row to join her. The theater was darkening, so Sarah did not notice my distracted state. I sank into my seat, clutching my unread program with trembling hands. It seemed ages before my heartbeat returned to normal and I was able to relax my frantic fanning. By then I'd decided upon an immediate course of action, and so I could actually concentrate.

But I wasn't concentrating on the stage in front of me. On another night Mamet's drama, focusing on the politics and pedagogy of faculty-student conferences, would have riveted me, but this night I was oblivious. My mind was on quite another tragedy. I was thinking of *Macbeth*.

Before leaving the theater, I made a quick phone call and then, thanking Sarah, I drove home.

Chapter 24

To: Menopausesupportgroup@powersurge.com
Subject: Time Out
Date: Thurs, 13 Dec 1994 23:45:16
From: Bbarrett@circle.com

What I'm struck by again is how little time I really make for the kind of relaxation and contemplation I crave. Sometimes, like tonight, for example, I couldn't even go to the bathroom in peace. Remember how it was when the kids were little? There was a period of three or four years when I almost never got to go to the bathroom without one of my kids in there getting potty trained or wanting to be read to or fed or cuddled. Well, to be a good teacher, one simply must have time to reflect on what goes on in the classroom and on what students write and how they write it. And Germaine Greer says that during middle age a woman makes the transition from "reproductive animal" to "reflective animal." How can I accomplish this metamorphosis if I still can't even go to the bathroom in peace?

And so my day ended where it had begun, in the kitchen. After I'd thrown off my coat, I sat at the counter, now lit by moonlight. Trembling slightly, I switched on the light, taking comfort in the room's ordinariness and familiarity. Silently I blessed Virginia Woolf, who was curled up in a large fruit bowl beside the newspaper. I filled the coffee pot with decaf and water and turned it on. Then I set the tea kettle to boil. Next I carefully removed the tape recorder from my purse, setting it gently on the countertop and clearing a space around it. Only then did I sit down to wait for Illuminada and Betty.

They arrived together. My finger to my lips, I cautioned, "Sol's asleep. Let's stay in the kitchen. We won't wake him if we talk back here."

"I don't know about this getting out of bed in the middle of the night to come traipsing over here. I don't give up my beauty sleep for anything, girl. Do you have any idea what time it is? This better be good. You serving breakfast?" In spite of her light tone, Betty's face, sagging with sleep, looked grim as her eyes traveled over my features. "Hey, you don't look so good."

Grinning, Illuminada flashed open her wool-lined trench coat to reveal the long blue flannel nightgown, demure except for a plunging neckline, that was all she wore beneath it. "*Caramba!* And I thought it was a pajama party! Surprise!" As Illuminada playfully pirouetted around the counter, tossing her coat on a chair, she too scrutinized my face. Pouring herself a cup of decaf, she sassed, "Bel, this looks like a nice place, but let's skip the house tour tonight, okay?"

We hunched over our warm mugs as, in a heightened whisper, I began to recap the events that had inspired me to convene the group despite the hour. Until I got to the part where I recognized the voices of the male intruders in the men's room, they had been amused. However, by the tale's end, both Betty and Illuminada sat still and silent, their eyes focused on the tiny tape recorder, suddenly conspicuous, as if aglow, on the cluttered countertop.

"Bel," began Illuminada, her whisper squeaky with anxiety, "just tell us how you got out of there without them seeing you. They didn't see you, did they?"

"I hope not. I mean, I don't think so, but I don't know for sure. I waited till the usher flickered the lights in there to signal the play was starting, and then I counted to one hundred. Then I held my breath and bolted for my seat. I didn't notice anyone around. Anyway, once I got out that door, anyone who noticed me would have assumed I was coming from the ladies' room. It's right next door."

Betty raised her coffee cup in a mock toast, "Here's to Bel." Sotto voce she added, "And her bladder." The three of us smiled, and I reached to turn on the tape recorder.

Illuminada blocked my arm, saying, "If you have another tape recorder in the house, let's record a backup so we'll have two tapes. That way if we mess one up, we'll still have the evidence. Actually, now that I think about it, I keep a pretty good recorder in the car. It's a tool of the trade. Want me to get it?"

"Yes," I answered gratefully. "The only other one we have is very beat up." While Illuminada, accompanied by Betty, was retrieving the tape recorder, I transferred a package of Sara Lee Danish from the freezer to the microwave, muttering to myself, "Desperate times call for desperate measures, right?"

Illuminada's big machine quite dwarfed my mini model. I hoped my tiny device that had always served so well in the classroom had proved equally reliable in the bathroom. "Here goes." I pressed rewind. "We'll probably have to listen to a minute or two of

Rosa Chavez's speech on Chilean *arpilleras* as feminist art. But it was very good. She had excellent visual aids too . . ."

"*Como mierda*, Bel! Shut up and hit play." We huddled closer around the counter, the better to catch every nuance.

". . . were a special type of protest that was not physically violent. But *arpilleristas* were still very effective in confronting the dictatorship. They fought an artistic, emotional and cultural kind of revolution. Thank you." We drew our small circle even closer as we stared at the little black box, willing it to continue.

". . . lease renewals went through with no problem, right? . . ." I exhaled with relief as the others strained to make out the conglomeration of noises and words: what sounded like running water, voices, zips, voices, footsteps, voices, more running water, more voices, and the final whoosh. It was all there, less audible than Rosa's exposition, but clear enough. I pressed stop and waited for a reaction. Automatically I began to serve the defrosted Danish.

Betty sounded worried. "Nobody knows about this tape but us, right? You don't want those dudes doctoring up your Danish, do you? We better go to the police. This sounds like a motive to me. You need protection." She gulped. "Now that we've all heard it, I guess we all need protection."

Illuminada interjected, "Calm down, Betty."

"Don't tell me to calm down, girl. Do you know I got a pink slip in the mail this week? That means they're not going to renew my contract, which ends in June. Since Lord Nelson can't wipe his butt without me to tell him where it is, I figure they're onto me for having Xeroxed the files. Either that or Tarantello has somebody lined up for my job too. That dude's got a big family. And I've got Randy's tuition to pay. So don't you tell me to calm down." Betty was still whispering, but she sounded angry and scared.

Illuminada spoke slowly as if she were thinking aloud, "I'm sorry, *chiquita*. I didn't know about the pink slip. I guess that's why I got a letter from the state questioning my gun permit. And, now that I think of it, Mamoud left me a message saying the class he asked me to teach next semester's been canceled. I'll have to check that on the spring schedule printout. Last month he was all over me to teach two classes, and now all of a sudden he doesn't even have one. Interesting, no? At least you have tenure, Bel. They can't do anything to you."

"They can't fire me without a fight, but you should see my spring schedule. My department chair, Joe Fink, just changed it into the schedule from hell. Now I understand why. He's always done what he was told. I guess they figure I'll butt out of this if they make my life miserable enough. That's the way their minds work. Well, they've got me all wrong."

Illuminada still looked worried. She said, "Don't be so sure. As of now, we can show they were motivated, all right, but not their method. How in hell did they do it? The only evidence still points to Oscar Beckman. And who is Jenkins? I'm going to send the original of this recording to a tape analyst I worked with once in upstate New York. Maybe he can eliminate the sound of the water. That should help."

I felt myself flush while Illuminada was talking. Still in a whisper, I said, "I think I was actually talking with Koladnar right after he did it. We were outside. He must have poisoned her just seconds before."

"What are you talking about?" Betty asked.

"During the Fall Festival I had a hot flash and left

the terminal to cool off by the river. I saw Koladnar leave the terminal wiping his glasses, except he wasn't wiping his glasses. Actually, I'm now certain he was wiping the cyanide vial clear of his fingerprints and wrapping a napkin around it. I'd seen the familiar wiping motions from a distance and assumed he was cleaning his glasses. I wasn't wearing mine. They were new and I wasn't quite used to them. Anyway, he was surprised to see anyone out there, but he made a nice recovery and came over and chatted with me, cool as a cucumber. He even offered me his jacket, which must have had the vial in the pocket. I mean, what if I'd put on his jacket and accidentally put my hand in the pocket? The damn thing would've had my fingerprints on it. But, of course, I wasn't cold. He went in after a few minutes, probably so he could be on the scene when Dr. G collapsed."

There was silence as the three of us contemplated my words. Then I continued, "I'm pretty sure he wanted to be there so they could incriminate Oscar Beckman. I figured out how they did that. When Lady Macbeth wants people to think the guards murdered the king, she smears blood on them while they're asleep. Well, that's kind of what Koladnar and Tarantello and maybe even Danzig did to Oscar."

"But there was no blood," said Betty.

"And this isn't Shakespeare," added Illuminada with a touch of impatience.

"Yes, but remember how everybody was pushing and shoving to clear space around Dr. G when she was lying on the floor, to give her air and make room for the paramedics? Oscar remembers Koladnar and Tarantello knocking into him especially hard, and he said he was sure they didn't mean anything by it.

Well, that's when Koladnar slipped the cyanide vial into Oscar's pocket."

Betty was the first to speak, "Altagracia worked so closely with each of them too. Who would have suspected that Tarantello had the smarts or the guts? Anyway, who could take him seriously? And the commissioner . . . Who'd have thought he cared that much? We thought he was trying so hard to get the governor to bend on the budget. And I guess he was. The more state money we get, the more jobs he can give out. I actually voted for him in the last election . . . and so did Altagracia." As she uttered the name of her dead friend, Betty's eyes filled.

I reached over the counter to pat her arm. Someday when there was time, I'd have to think about how I'd gradually grown close to Betty in spite of her prickly and pushy facade. "Remember, Betty, even though this evidence won't bring Dr. G back, it may save Andreas from a few years on the couch. He'll never have to learn about his dad's thing with Linda now."

"Just let me get this straight." Illuminada's voice was soft, but her diction was precise. "Koladnar slips cyanide either onto the victim's plate or into her glass. He goes outside, wipes off the empty vial, talks with Bel, and then goes back in. When Dr. Garcia collapses, there's a lot of confusion and everybody's pushing and shoving other people out of the way. During this melee, Tarantello distracts Oscar Beckman by pushing and shoving him while Koladnar puts the cyanide vial into the kid's jacket pocket. Since no one knows there has been a murder yet, the victim is taken to the hospital where she's pronounced dead. And before learning that there's been a homicide, a clean-up crew clears the scene, inadvertently destroying any other clues. The cops do background checks on everybody who had access to her food and drinks, especially the CAI students who were serving, and they come up with Oscar's suspension, his juvenile offenses, and his threatening letter. They check out CAI lockers and find Oscar's jacket with the vial in the pocket. Is that the same picture everybody else sees?" Illuminada looked up, seeking confirmation of the latest version of events.

Betty had regained her composure and was jotting notes even as she answered, "Yes. And as I see it, we need to go back into those files and pull out everything we can on Dworkin and the other owners of those leased buildings. And on Commissioner Thomas Koladnar and board president Dominic Tarantello." The venom in her voice was scary as Betty spit out the killers' names.

"You got it," Illuminada replied. "And don't forget Jenkins. Does that name mean anything? We have to see who Jenkins is and how he fits in. Let me think about all this for a day or two before we involve the cops or before we let Javier off the hook. *Dios mio*, now we have to consider really carefully who to talk to. It's way too sensitive now for the local cops. They'll never arrest Koladnar, let alone the others. We'll probably have to go to the State Police with the whole thing all tied up in a ribbon. Can you live with this for another couple of days before we go public?"

# Chapter 25

To: Menopausesupport@powersurge.com
Subject: New doctor!
Date: Fri, 16 Dec 1994 18:54:32
From: Bbarrett@circle.com

Good news! This afternoon after class I kept my appointment with Dr. Allison Bodimeind. I was tempted to postpone because I'm so stressed out and distracted now by a whole lot of things I can't even talk about. But I made myself get on the PATH and find my way to her office in Soho. I liked her a lot. I was a little put off at first because she's very young, probably not yet forty, but she has all the right certificates on her walls, and since Sophia recommended her so highly, I tried to keep an open mind.

She listened carefully and asked a lot of questions. She wrote down almost everything I said. Best of all, even though there were a lot of people waiting, she didn't rush me. I felt I could really talk to her, so I did.

When I told her about my mother's two mastectomies and my fears and confusion about hormone replacement therapy, she understood my questions. She said that research indicates no conclusive link between a family history of breast cancer and increased risk of taking low dosages of HRT, especially if one does annual mammographies and frequent self-exams. In fact, she's much more worried about my family's history of osteoporosis and heart disease. What she finally said was, "The years after fifty are the most creative time of a woman's life! If you were my mother, I'd put you on estrogen right now. I've already got her on it. And when I'm menopausal, I plan to be on it myself." She said I could try either pills or a patch, and I opted for the patch to start with. It seems less invasive.

Maybe, as Germaine Greer says, I'm a victim of a capitalist conspiracy against crones, but if I don't have to endure hot flashes, panic attacks, sleeplessness, mood swings, joint pain, heart disease, bone loss, and dry eyes and other body parts, I'd rather not, thank you very much. After work on Monday, I'm going to the pharmacy to pick up my patch.

Sol had been after me all week to check out that addition to the building on nearby River Street. He wanted me to see for myself the site that was to be the subject of the Citizens' Committee to Preserve the Waterfront meeting Monday night. And since Sol had been very patient with me lately, I wanted to gratify him. At the end of a semester I'm never real easy to live with, but since my impromptu taping session, I had been doing an especially convincing imitation of the proverbial basket case. Sol knew something was up, but he had refrained from asking me direct questions, so I hadn't lied to him. But I hadn't told him about the tape either. He would have wanted us to go straight to the authorities, and we weren't quite ready to do that yet.

So after work on Monday I decided to kill several birds with one stone and stop at our pharmacy, which was also on River Street for my estrogen patch and then walk by the construction site on my way home.

I was in for a surprise. Actually I was in for several surprises.

Surprise number one was that my pharmacy itself was the construction site Sol had been wanting me to see. Since my last visit, a nearly complete four-story addition had sprouted above our neighborhood drugstore. Each story swelled with a bay window, hallmark of all new Hoboken condos. The formerly trim one-story old brick-front building was now an eyesore, effectively walling off a small but very real sliver of skyline and sunshine.

It was hard to believe I hadn't noticed this happening, but I hadn't set foot in the place since last spring when Sol's bout with bronchitis had called for an antibiotic. Passing by in the car, I hadn't registered the change in the building's height. Before going in, I checked the address with the one on the slip of paper Sol had given me. Indeed, this was 242 River Street, the project CCPW was rallying us to protest.

Sol had explained that the druggist who owned the building was also a developer who wanted to cash in on the latest Hoboken condo craze by building over his store. He'd neglected to apply for a building permit, which would have required a zoning variance. The area on that side of the street is zoned exclusively for one-story commercial buildings. To even be considered for a variance, the owner would have had to provide parking for the new residents. Also, CCPW routinely protested waterfront construction that was not part of Hoboken's still murky long-range plan for developing our own strip of what realtors once again were dubbing New Jersey's "gold coast."

Surprise number two was Frank O'Leary's freckled face grinning at me from behind the counter. I'd always assumed that he worked in a pharmacy in Jersey

City, but I had been wrong. One of the best parts of living in the area where I teach is running into students where I least expect to find them. And believe me, I had certainly not expected Frank to be part of my estrogen patch acquisition plan, but there he was, all six feet of him, falling all over himself to be of service. "Yo, Professor Barrett. Hope you're not sick. Getting ready for the holidays? Did you give me my A yet? Seriously, can I help you with something?"

"Hi Frank. No, I'm not quite in holiday mode yet. And thanks, I'm fine, but I do need to get this filled," I said, ignoring the reference to his grade. I handed him my patch prescription matter-of-factly and, I hoped, without changing my facial expression.

"No problem," said Frank, taking the scrap of paper and, in one smooth motion, turning around and passing it to the white-coated man behind the next counter. "You want to wait?" Frank turned again to the pharmacist in the rear, asking, "How long for this one?"

"About fifteen minutes."

I barely registered the pharmacist's reply because surprise number three was a biggie. I just stood there, my mind a whirl of data synthesizing without any conscious effort on my part. "You sure you're okay, Professor? You want to sit down?" Frank was leaning toward me as he spoke. Then he flipped up a panel in the counter and came out, motioning to one of the two chairs conveniently situated for people who had to wait.

"You can have a seat and wait, or if you want, I can deliver it. Whatever you say." Frank looked really worried now, so I tried to focus on my reply.

"Gee, Frank, if it's not too much trouble, I would love for you to deliver it. I have a few more errands to run, so why not drop it off in about an hour. Is that okay?'' When Frank nodded, I scribbled my address on a Post-it, flashed him what I hoped was a reassuring smile, and left.

I rushed home and dialed directory assistance for 800 numbers. The operator gave me the number for New Jersey Poison Control Center right away. When I told the concerned party who took my call that I was an author writing a mystery and needed some advice on poisons, he calmed down. He wasn't too busy, he assured me. In fact, he sounded eager to be diverted from an uneventful stint at the phones. While I picked his brain, I took notes, not trusting myself to remember even the simplest recipe. When I finished grilling him, he was pleased to give me his name so I could acknowledge his help when my book was published.

As soon as I got off the phone, I put on a pot of coffee and a kettle of hot water. In the microwave I defrosted some homemade brownies I kept for emergencies. This was definitely an emergency. At the very thought of what I was about to discuss with Frank, I began to sweat. But by the time he arrived, my fan was doing its job, a plate of brownies waited on the kitchen counter, and the smell of fresh-brewed hazelnut coffee wafted through the house. I prayed Sol would not come home while Frank and I were talking.

"Hi, Professor Barrett. This place is awesome. Here's your prescription. You wanna sign here?'' Frank was looking around, taking in Sol's piano, the floor-to-ceiling bookshelves, the row of miniature china shoes on the mantlepiece, and Virginia Woolf, who was boldly inspecting his hightops. Like most students, he was clearly fascinated by this chance to observe me in my natural habitat. ''Excuse me for saying so, Professor, but you looked kind of funny before in the store. Are you sure you're okay?"

"Thanks, Frank. Yes, I'm really fine, just a little worried is all. There's something important I need to ask you about. Can you spare a few minutes? May I offer you a brownie and a cup of coffee?" I felt my face warming again at the prospect of involving Frank in the investigation. I didn't want to put him at risk. He was a student, after all. But he was also a friend of Oscar Beckman's and a criminal justice major, a future law enforcement officer himself.

"Yeah, if it's no trouble. Thanks." Frank took off his jacket, and I hung it on the coat rack. He kept his green baseball cap on and stood there awkwardly waiting for me to direct him to a chair. As I ushered him into the kitchen, I realized that Frank and I were so used to communicating in classes and conferences over papers that without written words between us we were both a little shy.

After I poured his coffee and fixed my tea, I passed him the brownies. "Frank, I just want to ask you a couple of questions about your job, okay?" When Frank looked up, momentarily distracted from his brownie, I took his glance to be acquiescence. "Tell me, didn't you once say that your boss is named Jenkins?"

"Yeah. Richard Jenkins. He owns the place. That was him there this afternoon. He's also got another registered pharmacist that comes in sometimes."

"Tell me also, didn't you mention something about dead rats? You once said, I think, that you found dead rats out back, right?"

Frank grimaced and said, "Yeah. Old man Jenkins said they were drawn out of the surrounding buildings when the work started upstairs. He put out rat poison. All I know is I had to put on gloves and bag those suckers so they could go in the trash. I had to do this two or three mornings. Then it stopped."

Now I was leaning over the table toward Frank, "Do you recall when you found those dead rats? I mean, was it in the summer or after school started? Can you remember?"

"Yeah. It was after, in the early fall right after I started working there, right around when they started working on the building."

"More coffee? Another brownie? Frank, can you remember anything unusual about Richard Jenkins's behavior back then when the project started? I mean, like his hours. Did he come in early or leave late? Get any strange deliveries? Anything like that?"

"Well, I don't know how strange this is, but not long after I first started working for him he stayed late a couple of times. Said he had to do some bookkeeping one time. Another time he said he wanted to do the inventory. I thought it was a little weird because he has a part-time bookkeeper. It's not like the place is so busy that he wouldn't have time to do the inventory during regular store hours. But I didn't say anything. I just work there. Now that I think about it though, he doesn't stay late anymore."

"Frank, do you remember if the mornings you found the dead rats were the mornings after he stayed late?"

"Not offhand I don't remember. But I'll think about it. You know, you said something before about did he get strange deliveries. I do remember that one afternoon he got a delivery from Animal House, you know, the pet store uptown? He said it was a gerbil for his kids. I thought it was odd to have it delivered to the store, but you never know. Maybe he wanted to surprise them."

"Did you actually see the gerbil?"

"No, come to think of it. He received the box and put it in back. I left before him that day and next day the box was gone. Professor Barrett, do you think Jenkins is mixed up in some drug scam or something?"

"Frank, I promise you that as soon as I have the answer, I'll tell you why I've been questioning you like this. Right now, the less you know, the better off you are."

"Professor, that is so corny, I can't believe you said it." I was relieved to see Frank grin as he stood to leave. He ran into Sol on the doorstep. My timing had been perfect.

That night I went with Sol to the CCPW meeting in the back room of McMahon's, an old gin mill around the corner, one of the few Hoboken bars that had resisted gentrification. Thanks to Jerry McMahon's generosity and concern for preservation, CCPW always met there. McMahon's back room was itself a classic worthy of preservation. The very air there was redolent with decades of stale cigarette smoke and spilled beer. By the time we left, the distinctive aroma had permeated even our underwear.

Marlene Proletariat, crusading president of Citizens' Committee to Preserve the Waterfront, stood on a chair and spoke loudly, "This part of River Street is zoned for one-story commercial buildings. Building Inspector Ratstein came to the Zoning Board meeting where Jenkins's application for a retroactive variance was being considered and explained that 'someone' in his office had made a mistake and issued Jenkins a building permit before he had even filed for the variance." With a nod toward the one reporter in the room, Marlene trumpeted, "This addition will ruin the river view for many and change the Main Street USA look and feel of our neighborhood. It will create more parking and traffic flow problems. The Zoning Board's approval process is a travesty and this project is an abomination."

Even as Marlene climbed down from the chair, I was bursting to tell her and the assembled group to relax. Jenkins would soon be out of commission for a long time. But I somehow managed to keep my mouth shut, especially when I realized that regardless of Jenkins's fate, it was highly unlikely that the new construction would be demolished. We had to keep this from happening again. I was unusually antsy throughout the rest of the meeting. I just couldn't wait to meet with Betty and Illuminada and share what I had learned.

Chapter 26

Fax: #344-555-4116
To: Bel Barrett
From: Sarah Wolf
Date: December 19, 1994

Bel, I interviewed Linda Allen today and learned, among other things, that on the evening of the festival at the time in question, she was being approached by Sid Schiff, who runs two galleries, one in New Hope and one in Philadelphia. He was impressed by her work and wants to mount a show and represent her. AND she got a fellowship to study in Florence this coming summer. Read all about her on the front page of next Sunday's arts section. Hope this is helpful. Remember our deal.

Fortunately I only had to wait until the next afternoon for Betty and Illuminada to come to my house. Sol was out, so we could talk freely. Betty got there first, looking tired and drawn. Just as I settled her in with a cup of Soothing Moments herbal tea, Illuminada came in also looking a little peaked. Betty spoke first, her voice plaintive and nasal, a far cry from her usual brisk businesslike patter. "So, what were you so excited about on the phone? I just want this to be over. Can you make it go away?"

Illuminada held up a piece of paper, saying, "I can't make it go away, but I can fill in some blanks. Thanks to the right-to-know laws we have here in this blessed country, I got a list of contributors to Koladnar's '92 campaign. Listen to this.'Helen Danzig, $2,500 cash; Roth, Gaffolino, and McLaughlin Associates, $5,000 cash—' "

"Hold on," I interrupted. "Who the hell are they?"

Betty spoke up, her voice steady but dull. "Bet the rest of Randy's tuition that's the consulting firm doing the site search, right?"

"You got it, *chiquita*," said Illuminada and continued to read, " 'Tarantello Brothers Container Company, $5,000 cash.' Even Sam Dworkin and Maxine Ratstein are down here for making an in-kind contribution of a site for Koladnar's downtown campaign headquarters."

Betty spoke again in the same dull tone. "Okay, okay. We get the picture. Now can you make it go away?"

"I can." I was amazed at how matter-of-fact I sounded. "I mean, this time I really can. Get this." We were seated around the counter in the same positions we'd assumed the other night when we'd listened to the tape. "Jenkins is Richard Jenkins, pharmacist-developer. He owns a drugstore on River Street here in Hoboken. To make a long story short, he needed a zoning variance to put up four stories of river view condos on top of his little store. Paul Ratstein, Hoboken building inspector, traded him the variance in return for some poison."

Illuminada interrupted me, sputtering, "*Dios mio!*

How do you know that? Did you sneak into the men's room in the drugstore too?"

"No, been there, done that," I quipped. "But I did do some sleuthing on my own." I have to admit I was bragging a little. "When I was in the pharmacy yesterday, I ran into Frank O'Leary, a student of mine who works there. He's a really good student, analytical, concise—"

Betty groaned, "Skip the case study, girl. Come on."

"Okay, so while Frank was waiting on me, a couple of things he said during the semester sort of swam back into my head. I arranged to meet him later to question him. Then I rushed home and called the Poison Control Center. I haven't talked to them since Mark's lips turned green when he was three. They're the ones who clued me in that Mark had probably eaten food coloring. They were right. He—"

"*Como mierda*, Bel! Cut the crap. Get on with it." Illuminada sounded mad.

"Right. Sorry. Anyway, I learned a few things. Pure cyanide is not readily available anymore except in Agatha Christie books. It's not even used for rat poison now. But a lethal cyanide brew can be made by dissolving the compound lead cyanide in water and pouring that into a drink."

Betty's mouth was working and she looked like she might be sick. Illuminada put her arm around her and signaled me to go on. "Jenkins had to practice to be sure he got the proportion right, so he used rats he had delivered from the local pet store. My student Frank saw one such delivery come in. Presumably there were a couple of others. Once Jenkins got the right proportion to kill a rat, all he had to do was multiply. Frank recalls having to throw out a few dead rats that appeared behind the store around the same time the construction started in late summer. Jenkins told Frank that the construction made the rats surface, and he poisoned them. But that kind of construction is clean and above ground. It's not the kind that brings out rats. That usually happens when there's demoliton or digging, like when they built Newport Mall. Remember? Those of us who live downtown in Hoboken and Jersey City were up to our ears in rats then."

"Bel, get on with it, please," Illuminada chided me.

"There's not a whole lot more. Ratstein and Jenkins made a deal. Ratstein gave him a building permit and smoothed the way for a belated variance if necessary, and Jenkins provided the poison."

"What's in it for Ratstein?" I was relieved to hear Betty chime in, her words clipped once more.

"Ratstein is Sammy Dworkin's brother-in-law, remember? Sammy's sick and wants to keep his lease with RECC going and to get his son hired. And that's probably just the start of his wish list. Who knows? He might even want to be the next RECC president."

I kept my promise. After Illuminada called the State Police, I called Sarah Wolf.

Chapter 27

**COMMISSIONER AND BOARD BIGWIGS CHARGED
IN POISONING OF RECC PRESIDENT**
Koladnar, Tarantello, and Ratstein
held without bail pending indictment
by Sarah Wolf

State troopers joined Jersey City and Hoboken
officers in a police action resulting in the arrest last
night of several prominent local leaders in connection
with the poisoning death of Dr. Altagracia Garcia, late
president of River Edge Community College. The
police acted in response to information supplied by
Illuminada Guttierez, a private investigator working
on behalf of the victim's family and friends. Dr.
Garcia was pronounced dead on arrival at Jersey City
Medical Center on the night of Friday, October 14,
after she collapsed at a college fund-raising event.
RECC student Oscar Beckman had been charged with
her murder.

Arrested at their homes late last night were
Thomas Koladnar, Jersey City Commissioner of
Finance; Dominic Tarantello, president of the RECC

Board of Trustees and director of the Jersey City Sewage and Water Authority; Paul Ratstein, member of the RECC Board of Trustees and Hoboken's building inspector; and Richard Jenkins, local developer and owner of Miles Square Pharmacy. All are being held without bail in the county jail pending arraignment. None of their attorneys returned this reporter's calls requesting interviews or comment.

Guttierez indicated in a brief statement to the press that recent hirings and leasing agreements at the college were now the subject of scrutiny in view of RECC's long history of patronage and the evidence submitted that led to the arrests. She also confirmed that charges against Oscar Beckman have been dropped. In view of these developments, the future of the college is uncertain.

The Beckman family threw a big bash on New Year's Day to celebrate Oscar's exoneration. I arrived late because first Mark wanted to chat about the meaning of life over brunch. Then Rebecca wanted me to hit the Tenth Street Baths with her for a soak and a massage, and Sol decided we should all meet at the Angelika to see *Il Postino* afterward. So the Beckmans' party was in full swing by the time I got there.

The guest of honor was resplendent once more in his uniform of black-and-white checked pants and crisp white jacket. Taking my arm, Oscar led me into the room. "Professor Barrett, I'd like you to meet my mom," he said as he placed an arm around a plump, smiling woman. "Ma, this is the professor I been tellin' you about, the one who helped get me off and who helped get the guys who really killed the president."

Tears filled Mrs. Beckman's eyes, making it a struggle for her to speak. "You're a saint. I knew he never poisoned nobody. The nerve a them thinkin' my Ozzie done somethin' like that. He's a good boy. Always been a big help to us in the deli."

"Well, Mrs. Beckman," I replied, "I knew Oscar didn't do it too, but I had lots of help figuring out who did. Have you met Betty Ramsey and Illuminada Guttierez?" I scanned the room in search of my accomplices.

"Yeah. Ozzie introduced me and his father to them two before. We don't know how to thank you for what you done for Ozzie. Now the cops even got the guy who got the poison. Can you believe the nerve? The druggist who owns Miles Square Pharmacy in Hoboken traded poison to the building inspector for a permit to build on top of his store!" Mrs. Beckman rolled her eyes. "And the commissioner too? He's the one actually put the poison in her drink. And that SOB stuck that bottle in my Ozzie's jacket." Mrs. Beckman paused, new tears misting her eyes.

"Mrs. Guttierez and Mrs. Ramsey was tellin' us how they got the guy what tried to hurt you too." Shaking her head, Mrs. Beckman continued to recite the now familiar story. "This punk's uncle, Dominic Tarantello, and the commissioner put him up to it, Ozzie says. They heard about the letter you wrote for Ozzie and that you was meetin' with him. They got the punk to wait for you in the park and run you down and later they got the same punk to mess wid the brakes of your car. And then they give the punk a big job at the college makin' like fifty grand a year. You know, Professor—"

"Excuse me, Mrs. Beckman," Wendy said, interrupting. "Bel, I need to borrow Oscar for just a minute. And Bel, could you use that foghorn voice of yours to get a little quiet in here? I'd like to make an announcement."

I knew what was coming, so I was glad to rap on a glass and bellow, "May we please have your attention." Gradually a hush fell. Climbing on a chair, Wendy proclaimed, "Oscar, your children's cookbook, *Kids Can So Cook*, has won the Hearthstone Press contest, and they plan to publish it next spring!"

Mrs. Beckman looked a bit addled, and then a smile brightened her face. Oscar's lips twitched and his eyes filled. Oh God, was he going to cry? He wouldn't want to do that here. I let out my breath when Oscar threw his arms around his mother and tried to get up on the chair to hug Wendy. People were clapping and someone proclaimed yet another toast.

Then Oscar recognized Frank O'Leary and his girlfriend on the other side of the deli and made his way over to them through the crowd of well-wishers. I followed, eager to meet Frank's girl, thank him for his help, and congratulate him on his stellar *Macbeth* paper. "Frank, how good to see you here."

Frank nodded in the direction of the pretty, dark-haired girl at his side. "Professor Barrett, this is Terri. Terri, my prof."

As Terri and I shook hands, I said to Frank, "Well, Frank, if you need a letter of recommendation when you transfer to State, I'll be happy to write one on the basis of your paper alone. It is quite interesting."

A grin flashed across Frank's face and then quickly disappeared. He straightened his shoulders and, looking at Terri, said, "Well, I'll take a raincheck on that. I've decided not to transfer yet. I'm going to finish up here part-time before I go to State."

Since I'd known him, Frank had been planning to

transfer to State at the end of the semester. What could have made him change his plans?

As if in answer to my unasked question, Terri spoke up softly, solemnly, "Professor, Frank and I are getting married next month. We're sending you a wedding invitation."

Frank put his arm around Terri, who was gazing up at him, her deep-set hazel eyes agleam with adoration. "Yeah. We're, I mean, Terri's expecting. In August." As he spoke, Frank's freckles were almost obliterated by the blush that reddened his face. His arm tightened around Terri's waist.

In the face of their revelation and youthful romanticism, I found myself troubled. Silently I hoped that they would sustain their lovers' glow through the many struggles sure to come. I also hoped that they would both be able to continue college. But rather than share these sentiments, I gave each of them a big hug and said, "Well, congratulations and my very best wishes to you both. State's loss is RECC's gain. I'll be watching the mail for that wedding invitation."

Over Terri's shoulder I spotted Sarah Wolf, camera in hand. Now managing editor at the paper, Sarah was trailing Oscar in the hope of arranging an interview. Sarah's promotion had followed her scoop about who really killed Dr. G.

"Have ya had somethin' ta eat?" Mrs. Beckman suddenly shifted roles, abandoning her mother-of-the-unjustly-accused persona for the much more comfortable one of hostess at Bayonne's premier deli. The overjoyed and relieved Beckmans had gone all-out. Fresh mozzarella, antipasto, eggplant parmigiana, homemade sauerkraut, sauerbraten, and wursts of all sorts covered the buffet table. Also there was a splendid chocolate cake baked by Oscar's friends from culinary school with "Way To Go Ozzie!" splashed across its frosting in spun sugar script. They were there in force, serving food and drinks so the Beckmans could schmooze with guests.

As Mrs. Beckman turned to greet another late arrival, I slipped away to a corner booth where I'd glimpsed Betty and Illuminada quietly sipping champagne and demolishing a huge tray of antipasto that they'd commandeered to their table. I settled myself next to Betty and reached for a stuffed mushroom. Signaling one of the roving servers, I helped myself to a glass of champagne and sighed with contentment.

"So what's going down at RECC now that several members of the Board of Trustees and the acting president are under indictment? Who's minding the store?" asked Illuminada, with a twinkle in her eye. "Do you think I'll be able to teach at least one section next semester?"

Betty was quick to reply. "Good question. You know, I was all set to leave. I updated my résumé and everything." Betty was unusually subdued.

"Give me a break, Betty," I interrupted. "You can't leave now. There's no continuity in that office. If you're not there, who'll orient the next president? I heard the state is actually sending someone from Trenton to run the place until a new board is constituted and a new presidential search is completed. Can you imagine the chaos if you leave?"

"Oh, Betty." Illuminada couldn't resist teasing her. "You're used to being the only person who knows what's going on in that office. If you're not careful, you'll end up being the next president."

"Actually, that wouldn't be such a bad idea. Things would certainly get done," I added with a smile.

Betty was not amused. "Well, don't joke. When the accreditors find out that most of the board and maybe even the acting president and a local bigwig are being indicted for conspiring to poison the college's president, they just may decide to revoke our license. And who could blame them? Then we'll all be out of work."

I winced. "Oh God. The accreditors. I worry about them. I sure hope Dean St. Clair and the Faculty Senate can pull something off to appease them until we have a new board and a decent presidential search process in place."

"What about that new waterfront campus Altagracia wanted?" Now Betty sounded wistful.

Illuminada turned both her tiny thumbs down in an emphatic gesture. "Forget it. The waterfront will be a wall of offices and luxury housing from Hoboken to Fort Lee. Besides, there won't be any state money for this place for a long time. The governor and the other Republicans in the legislature are always looking for a reason to cut funding for higher education, and *Dios mio*, don't you think we've given them a good one? Who is there to lobby for our students now? No, there will be no new campus."

Betty looked as if she were about to cry when she said, "Yeah. Not only did they kill Altagracia, but they killed her dream too. Can you imagine how much was at stake for them to actually kill her? It's just so hard to believe."

"Hey, *chiquita*, when we talk about patronage here, we're talking about about people's livelihoods. There's a whole segment of the population supported for generations by patronage jobs. And these people support political types like your friend the comissioner, whose careers depend on their coming through with those jobs." Illuminada's voice was rising with her indignation, and her words poured out in an angry snort.

I had to add my two cents, so I said, "Yeah, it's part of the culture, like double parking. People don't see anything wrong with it. And add to that some of the hottest real estate in the entire country and, hell, people have killed for a lot less." I was on a roll. "And they don't care about anything except protecting their cash flow. They don't care if RECC is run well or if students get their education. To them, RECC's not a college, it's an employment agency. It doesn't have to have good facilities, it just has to employ people."

Betty broke in saying, "Altagracia sure wanted it to be a good college. She wanted great teaching, first-rate facilities, and top-notch support services. She thought nothing was too good for our students. I guess she was just in the way."

Illuminada sighed and said, "She sure was." We were all silent for a moment, and then Illuminada continued, "You know, I'm not even sure I want to come back in the fall. Since this story broke, my office phone's been ringing off the hook. What do I need to work for slave wages as an adjunct at RECC for?"

"Remember, you're the one who wanted to give something back?" I couldn't resist nudging Illuminada about her earlier altruism. Illuminada was turning out to be a dynamite teacher. She couldn't leave. I wanted Frank O'Leary to take her course.

"Hey, let's lighten up," said Betty, tapping on her glass with her ring. "We don't know what's going to happen in the long run. But we do know that next week students will be coming to begin the spring semester, so for now you two just better be in the classroom teaching, and I better be in my office telling the next acting president which end is up."

Automatically I reached for my fan. Only then did I realize that I wasn't sweating. "Hear, hear. I'll drink to that." We raised our glasses and downed the last of our champagne.

January 2, 1995

Eleanor Roosevelt University
An independent university educating people for democracy
School of Education
Office of Graduate Studies
John Dewey Hall
1 Reflection Square
New York, New York 10004

Dear Ms. Barrett:

We are pleased to inform you that your application for admission to the Doctor of Philosophy course in Program 444L (English Education: Applied Linguistics) has received preliminary approval. If you now wish to enroll in doctoral coursework on a "matriculation pending" basis, with no formal guarantee that you will ultimately be accepted for matriculation, please consult with Professor Gordon St. John in order to obtain approval to register for such coursework.

Professor St. John will discuss with you further submissions (GRE scores, for example) required in order that the Faculty Subcommittee on Doctoral Matriculation can consider your application. He will also advise you on other matters germane to your status as a "matriculation pending" student. Finally, he will help you select appropriate

courses for next semester and sign your registration form
so that you may register by computer.

We applaud your decision to attend graduate school and
wish you every success in your studies.

Sincerely,

Ms. Cecily Trench
Admissions Coordinator (212-555-2486)

cc: Professor Gordon St. John